BONES BOOK ONE

# Forest Empire

## by Jim Rudnick

RUDNICK PRESS

FE-CreateSpace

ISBN-13: 978-1-988144-18-4
Copyright © 2016
Jim Rudnick

# For my Susan...

## __Bones Book Two: Forest Empire...__

"Trapped by a tribe of slavers, Javor and his group fight their way free, only to find that one is never truly free. Engaged by the Regime to act as Ambassadors to the Forest Empire, they travel through more than a hundred miles of dense boreal forests only to be warmly received...and then betrayed.

Now slaves, the group is made to work on the building of the new Pyramid, by pulling huge stones to the building site and then up a ramp for construction—and the fact that the project is way behind makes the whips of the guards sting even more.

When faced with watching a youngster die or doing something, Javor chooses to save her life and in doing so a guard dies. That sentences Javor to the cult's Mid-Summer games where he will try to outrun the spears of the Shieldsmen—and live...or not..."

# A Message to you from the Author...

I just wanted to say thanks so so much for reading Book two of the Bones Series...

As my Amazon bio says, being a youngster in the 1950's meant that I was a voracious reader in what has been called the Golden Age of Science Fiction. That meant that for me, my heroes were not on the hockey rink or gridiron - but instead in my local Library where at 12 I had a full Adult card (thanks Dad!) and took out more than 5 books a week.

Everyone from Heinlein, Norton, Leiber, Pohl, Anderson, Simak, Asimov, Brackett, Gunn, Van Vogt and more....I fell in love with and eventually owned Ace Doubles of my own.

And while I never knew who wrote the Tom Corbett - Space Cadet series, I fell in love with them and they had a place of honor on my own bookcase too!

With that kind of an introduction to Science Fiction, it's no wonder that when I got my writing work done, I turned my own fictional side of my brain to writing same. It's one thing I know how to write - and a totally different matter to release same to the world - something that I've just started to work on....

Suffice it to say my own works are rooted in that Golden Age and it's that era that I'd like to one day be known as a teensy contributor to in some small way...

So once again, thanks for beginning my Bones series and wait'll you learn about the world that our hero lands on...

Enjoy and remember, in a series, characters develop and mature not the way we sometimes want...instead, it's like they have a life of their own!

# CHAPTER ONE

Thinking that a wakeup call that included banging a garbage can lid with a huge steel bar was about the worst he'd ever heard, Javor slowly rolled to his right and was stopped by the hip of the captive beside him. Slowly sitting up, he rubbed his face with both hands and thought too that lying and sleeping on a plank floor was far from comfortable. His right knee with its alien inserts was fine however, and he suffered none of the cramps that sometimes followed an uncomfortable night's sleep.

"Rise and shine, slaves. Brekkie in ten minutes, outside bathroom break for one and all—now," the tribe woman shouted, but she continued to bang against that lid at the same time.

He helped Sue up by an arm, and once everyone was up and on their feet, the woman turned and led

6

the way out of their room back into the barn. Joined by a couple of men with shotguns, she carried the big ring of steel that held all the smaller shackle rings and led the way out of the barn down a slope toward the fields. Only twenty feet or so later, she stopped and said, "Relief time—and I've heard it all before. Either pee here or don't—we don't care," and she slid down her leggings and squatted and peed for all to see.

Javor didn't like it, but then beggars—or rather, captives—can't be choosers. He slid open the fly on his jumpsuit and aiming straight down, he relieved himself too. He noted that both Wayne and Bruce had formed a bit of a shield for Sue, who squatted, and soon all were once again standing and waiting for breakfast.

When they came back into the barn, the woman with the big ring of steel led them to a short set of tables strung together. She took a foil plate and a plastic fork from the end of the table and then scooped up some eggs and what looked like fried baloney. She made her way slowly toward the hay bales stretched out on that side of the barn. She dropped the big ring with a clatter and took a seat on a bale, and as the captives slowly went through the line, she watched them only haphazardly.

Seems that they trust the shackles mostly, Javor thought. Good to know, and he checked off that shortfall in the tribe's security.

After the poor tasting eggs and what he now hoped had actually been baloney, he too tossed his plate and utensil over his shoulder back into the bales and looked around.

Most of the men must have already eaten as they were now packing up their supplies, and a couple of them were putting them into overstuffed backpacks. Every once in a while, one would whistle, and a woman would come to pick up a newly packed backpack and then drop it at one of the captive's sides.

Looks like we do the carrying, Javor thought, and he hoped for a light bag too.

In no more than twenty minutes, the packing was done, and each of the captives had been loaded up with a heavy backpack. Once again, the same woman led them out of the barn with the big steel ring threaded over her shoulder. She looked like she was about thirty with what looked like a big fresh tattoo that was scabbed over all across one of her breasts. While he couldn't tell exactly what it was, it was an animal of some kind. Her fingernails, he noted, were short and dirty, her leggings had stains on them, and her boots—if one could call them that—were in need of re-soling. That topknot of hair, in her case, was in need of a wash and a brushing at the least.

For a tribe, the women—at least these women, he thought—were very much an unkempt lot.

The men, however, were more the masters here. Each was dressed much better than the women were. Each topknot was shiny and some were braided very intricately too, he noted. Boots were leather and some looked newer than others. On the whole, men were in charge in this tribe—that was obvious.

As they all left the barn, Javor noted their detail. No one took point truly but three men, two with rifles, walked up front. Behind them came the women and then the captives, followed by the remaining few men. Counting, he saw there were two rifles and four shotguns that he could see. He could also see there were no other long arms at all, as they couldn't be hidden under a sash or a belt. One of the men at the front carried his own Colt— he could see that plainly, so it was a prize for sure. Sue's pistol he couldn't account for as yet, but it was still on someone in the group of fifteen tribe members. Only fifteen of them with six long guns and at least two handguns.

And we've got a single revolver—with only six rounds. Sounds like a fair fight, he lied to himself, and that got a shrug and a part smile. But what we do have is surprise. Add in the fact that this tribe appears to not be tactically adept—would mean that if we can divide, we can conquer. Over the next mile or so, he had the foresight to let his team know the word NOW meant they were going for it as surprise might work well with their captors. Anything they could lay their hands on to fight back with should be used.

The way ahead was pretty easy, as the captives were led down to Regional Road 17, and then they turned to the left, toward Arlington, Javor knew. He caught Sue's eye and they both pursed their lips, as they knew they were going to get closer to the Regime somehow. At least they were going in the right direction.

After more than three hours of steady walking on the regional road, the three men up at the front broke their pace and stopped at the side of the road. One of them—the leader as far as Javor knew— gave some orders to the rest of the tribe.

"Amal—you're in charge. Continue to Bossence, then take the left to go to Omni—just like always. We'll hunt and meet you at Omni—no mistakes. Do not lose any of our slaves either—each means money to the tribe. But do kill anyone who tries to escape," he finished off, and around Javor, some of the captives gasped.

He and two riflemen left the roadway then and went off at a trot toward the wood lots a half a mile away.

Amal, the one who was now in charge, went from the back of the grouping and led the way himself along with one of the shotgun men too. That meant one long gun up front and three behind. No visible handguns either.

Javor wondered how far it was to this next town called Bossence, so he asked, "How much further 'til I can pop a couple of blisters, please?" in a calm polite voice.

That got him a dirty look from the woman with the big steel ring around her shoulder and "Four miles which should pop 'em for you," and he knew it was an hour to Bossence, and they turned off the road toward Omni.

"Bossence is where we'll make our play," he whispered to Sue, and she passed on the whisper to Bruce and then to Wayne. He got a look from Wayne that seemed to say "here," and over the next few yards they walked, he and Wayne got closer with Sue moving up ahead and Bruce dropping back a little in the middle.

Wayne suddenly lifted up his left leg, while grabbing onto Javor's shoulder as he hopped a couple of steps, and Javor drew the pistol and stuffed it in his belt but around the back and under his shirt. Bruce had moved up to cover that, and Sue too had also begun hopping and said, "Cramps … Goddamn cramps," and she hopped a few more

11

times until she hobbled. By what they all saw, their subterfuge had worked.

Javor had the gun, no one had noticed the hand off, and they were less than an hour away from the town of Bossence.

How was the next issue. Four long guns and maybe a handgun to overcome ...

The walk was still fine along the farm country road; sunny and bright, and if one discounted the hulks of the burned cars and pickups now and then, almost pretty. Farmhouse after farmhouse went by, mostly white clapboard but a couple were the really older type made from red brick and two stories tall. Shutters were on every window, and front porches with settings of chairs were still in place. Driveways that held trucks and a few cars were seen every so often, and barns still looked picture perfect but had not been used in years. Out behind the occasional barn, one could see farming equipment, like combines and tractors, still parked waiting to be used again one day.

Going to be a long time coming, Javor thought as he continued to try to soak up as much of Bones as he could.

Ahead on the right, used for target practice, of course, a sign read Bossence: one mile away.

He knew they were veering off to the left once they reached Bossence, so the play needed to come then.

As they went past the Welcome to Bossence sign, the woman ahead took the big steel ring off her shoulders and rubbed the flesh there that was red. Each of the sub-chains and their connectors had worn a dent into her flesh, and each of them too looked like they hurt.

She carried the ring in her hand, and as they crested a small rise in the road, the downtown of Bossence beckoned.

There was angle parking with several abandoned cars. Garbage was all over the streets. Most of the glass in the various town shops had been long ago broken, and those shards lay everywhere. Cracks in the pavement and asphalt had led to growth of weeds, and in spots, it was pretty thick too, he noted. All in all, Bossence looked like any other small town on Bones … dilapidated, disheveled, and in disrepair.

As they got to the main intersection, the signs on the pole on the right corner read Regional Road 17 straight and County Road 5 to Omni, turn left. They turned left.

About a half block down, Sue called out. "Hey … I gotta go number two real bad—could we have a five-minute break?"

Her voice sounded pretty uptight, Javor thought. The woman at the head of the shackled captives stopped, sighed, and then nodded.

Bruce and Wayne looked around, and seeing some newspapers on the ground, they gathered some up for Sue to use and handed them to her.

"Gonna be loud and messy, it is," Sue said, and that got the woman upset.

"Hold it … hold it, everybody else sit," she said as she called out to the men behind them at the rear.

"Billy, come up here and cover these ones, will you? You other two look after the rest of the slaves," she said as she undid the connector between the sub-chain that held the four of them and the big steel main ring. She dropped the ring on the ground and then motioned for the four of them to follow her.

Sue led the way on their short shackles, followed by Javor and then Wayne and Bruce and well back, Billy and his shotgun.

They went down the street a few stores and past an empty lot, and at the edge of the line of storefronts, the woman poked her head into what had once been a women's clothing store, and after a quick look, she shoved Sue only inside the door.

"Here … get it over with," she said, and she motioned for them all to sit.

With only ten feet of chain, Sue did her best to get some privacy.

Javor watched Billy carefully.

Sue yelled from inside, "There's rats in here!" and the sounds of her scrambling on the tile floor carried outside.

The woman rose up as Billy got closer too, and Javor thought, NOW, and then he yelled, "Now!"

He half-turned against the wall of the store, drew the pistol, thumbed off the safety, and shot Billy once in the body. Billy went down, shotgun at his feet.

Bruce was closest and he used his ten feet of chain to frog leg over to the fallen tribe member, and he scooped up the shotgun right away.

Sue came out of the women's clothing store swinging, and down the tribal woman went after taking a solid right cross to the chin.

Out on the street, Amal and his man up front turned at the noise, and before the man with the shotgun could even raise it up, Bruce sprayed him twice and down he went.

Javor's attention was on the two shotguns behind them, and after leaning on the edge of the women's clothing store doorway and supporting the pistol properly, he put two shots into the one on the right who went down, shotgun flying away.

The sound of the other tribe member's shotgun returning fire was loud, and the blast got them all in some way.

Sue and Bruce got a couple of pellets in the arm.

15

Wayne was crouching down below the blast, and he suddenly rose up and threw a perfectly pitched rock right at the man with the shotgun.

Bixby suddenly charged right at the man, which was a big surprise. Where he'd come from and how he'd known to attack at that instant was hard to understand, but as he grabbed the man by the calf, he ripped and tore at his flesh.

The tribe member screamed, kicked Bixby off, grunted, and then knelt to re-load as Javor once again braced his arm with support and slowly squeezed off a shot and missed. Went high, he thought as he used his last shell to knock the man over, his shotgun not even loaded yet.

Score was us one, them zero … he thought, and then he took stock.

Among the captives were the four men, young men looking pretty fit, dressed in camouflage, who'd known what was going on. One of them had even been able to grab the shotgun, and he stood looking at them. He pumped the gun once, and out flew an unused shell, which he quickly reloaded.

Javor said quietly to his group, "Let's stand down. Chains first." He nodded at Sue who slowly went through the pockets on the leggings of the knocked-out woman who had led them so far.

"Got it," she said as she pulled out a single key and then undid first herself, then Javor, then

16

Wayne, and finally Bruce.

Javor nodded. "Bruce, collect the rest of the tribe, put 'em all in a single line across the street, and have them sit on the curb. And bring Amal to me when you're done, and search every one of them better than they did," he said, keeping the revolver covering as much of the tribe as he could.

He slowly walked over to one of the men in camouflage and handed him the key. "Unlock yourselves—everyone, please, if you would," and he got a nod back.

He went halfway across the street and looked at the tribe members all looking sullenly back at him. Amal stood alone and as Javor walked up to him, the tribe member shook his head.

"You have made a big mistake, slave. You have to answer to the Red Tribe—and to the Forest Empire too. We will lose much if we do not sell you all to them—and so you will pay for that one day in the future.

Sue came back from looking at the wounded. "One up front is dead, as is one of the ones at the back too. Other one back there," she said as she pointed at one who was rolling from side to side, moaning, "will not last the night. That, and with all this noise, I'm sure that there's zombies headed this way as well.

He nodded. Good thing to remember that

gunshots mean zombies are on their way.

He smiled at Amal. "Unlike you—we do not hold any animosity towards others. We will be on our way, and we will not take it kindly if we meet up with you again. The rest of the slaves—no, the captives—are also free to do as they wish. We're on our way to Lindos, and it's a free city, so you'd best hope that we don't meet you before we get there. Now sit," he said, and Amal did just that.

Sue was talking with the other captives who were rubbing their wrists where the chains had chafed their skin. "You are all free. You know now to stay away from this tribe, who we'd imagine will go on to Omni to meet up with their others. We're going to get going now …" she said, and she, Bruce, and Wayne joined Javor in the middle of the street.

One of the men dressed in camouflage said, "Care for any company?"

They all looked at each other. Sue shrugged and finally said, "Yes, anyone who'd want to go to Lindos, you can come along," and that got some nods from others just freed from slavery.

They quickly dumped out the backpacks they'd been forced to carry and from the contents took some MREs, fire-starting equipment, other food items, and utensils. In one backpack, there was ammo for the shotguns but none for the revolver.

Javor took point, smiled, and leaned over to

scratch Bixby behind the ears. "Good boy ... good dog, Bixby," he said, and he led the way down County Road 6 back toward the main intersection and then right toward Lindos.

Bruce held back just outside of town and waited a full half hour before he trotted up to the group of them moving east toward Lindos. "You were right, Javor—they went straight down the road toward Omni ... we're good, I'd think."

Javor nodded and called a halt. "To our guests— we lied back there. We're not going to Lindos—but this road does just that. In, what, thirty miles, you'll be there. We're on our way to Arlington, about the same distance but north of us here. Next county road, we're veering north—you can either continue on your own way to Lindos or come along on the hike to Arlington. Doesn't matter to us, one way or the other," he said, and that got them talking among themselves.

At the next county road, only a mile farther, he led the way off to the left and north and noted that only the four men in camouflage came along, one still carrying the shotgun too.

"There's a story," he said to himself, "and one that we'll hear tonight too, I'd think ..."

#####

After turning north again, on what was labeled

County Road 13, the small group had hiked along with a degree of speed that showed they were worried. Anxious, maybe, Javor thought, but not worried maybe.

They had lied to the Red Tribe and said they were going to Lindos—and most of the captives had continued on County Road 5 toward the free city. But at the next intersection, Sue and her group, along with the four men in camouflage, all turned north toward somewhere else.

They traveled on a long, long country road with scenery they'd all seen hundreds of times—dead overgrown farms and country road corners with the occasional gas station too. Each time they reached a station, they checked, of course, for any kind of power generators—solar or wind. All were unpowered, so there was no new group to meet.

"Wonder if we find one," Wayne said, "if they'll have a red hair dryer too?"

That got a laugh from the group—except for the camouflage-dressed members. "Red hair dryer?" one asked who'd drifted up and now walked alongside Wayne.

"We found a station a ways back that had big wind fans on the roof—that were turning. Inside, in the working cooler, there were caches of food and drinks—beers too! And a single red hair dryer charging too, we noted," he said as an explanation.

The guy in camouflage looked over at one of his compatriots and got a nod. "We've found same too. Not the hair dryer, mind you—but yeah, wind fans mostly though a couple of solar panels too—all running some kind of very local micro power to a single building or farmhouse or storefront.

"In one case, we found the place populated too—which ended badly for them. Smart zombies—armed and yet not so good at tactical firefights. They lost," he said, and all could hear that he was a bit proud of that result.

So far, they'd not talked much—that would be for later. It was good to know, Javor thought, that their experience seemed to be wider than they'd imagined.

As they traveled, they passed by many farms. Some were generations-old farms with red brick farmhouses. Others were newer with clapboard or siding. The barns ranged from still perfect condition to burned or half-wrecked. Most of the silos still stood as the tallest structures on the properties, yet some had fallen and laid in pieces around the barnyards.

Rarely, they passed by the farms that had supported more than one generation—where the sons and daughters had moved out of the farmhouse and had built a new dwelling alongside the road with its own driveway and outbuildings.

As they came down a slope off a minor hill behind them, Sue stopped and said, "We need to camp out tonight. I'd say, judging by the shadows, it's getting past dinnertime."

And she was right. As most of them looked to the west, they saw the sun was just now touching the horizon.

One of the men in camouflage asked, "Do we try one of these ranch houses for cover?" and he pointed to the two houses alongside the road.

Each had its own drive and each was yet still a part of the overall farm that ran on the right side of the road now for almost a mile. The farmhouse and barn area was back at least three hundred yards, so these two houses were somewhat alone. One of the ranch houses was brown—the first one in line—and the second one was white.

She nodded. "Let's try them both—same time. Shotguns in first—and if there's no surprises, then let's compare and take the best one. We'll need guard duty though too tonight," she offered.

The camouflage man with the shotgun nodded and then led his group of four over to the brown house, aligning with the front door, and then waiting until Bruce had taken up a similar position at the white ranch house farther down.

Sue nodded and then yelled, "GO," and the doors were kicked open and the leads entered the houses.

Javor stood on the porch of that second house, as he was unarmed—the damn revolver was empty—and waited.

Bruce called out, "Clear on the main floor."

Javor entered the house. Inside, it was obvious that the old occupants had been neat and tidy. Not a single thing was out of place. The living room had a big wood fireplace so they could have a hot dinner, he noted, as he went into the kitchen and stopped cold.

In front of him at the kitchen table sat a corpse of what might have been a man—or a large woman—dressed in tattered shirt and jeans. He had no way of knowing whether it had been a man or woman as the hair on the bare scalp was now thin and of indeterminate length. The face had long ago been eaten by something, and the hands jutting out of the cuffs of the flannel shirt had been chewed on, the fingers missing.

"Probably a victim of the virus bombs but fell to something else maybe?" Bruce offered as he looked on too.

There was no way to know, and Javor left the room with sadness—so many killed by the Boathi, all for naught. He tightened his grip on his gun and wished for a full magazine and a Boathi in front of him, but then he shook his head.

All gathered back in the living room, and Sue said, "Failing anything better than this, we should camp here—tell the camos, will you, Wayne?" and she took off her backpack and stretched.

After everyone had reconvened in the white ranch house, each one found a place to sit in the living room. It was a chore, Javor realized, trying to cook an MRE out of the package by using the pots and pans found in the kitchen, so he just ripped the tab on one labeled cabbage rolls and waited while the magnesium and water combined to warm the interior of the foil pouch. While he did that, he found that the Red Tribe had tossed out his dog food kibble, and he was stumped for a moment.

One of the men in camouflage was watching and noted Bixby sitting attentively waiting to be fed and Javor was empty handed. He grinned as he dug into his bag and came out with a foil wrapped brick of something.

"Figure that this might be helpful," he said as he carefully unwrapped what looked like a solid pound of some kind of air-dried meat.

"It was from about a month back—we came on a herd of stags, shot one, and ate like kings for a week. This was air-dried to keep it still edible, and if you heat it up in some water, it should feed killer here just fine." He tossed the meat over.

Javor looked at it carefully. He pulled out his

knife from behind his armored vest and realized the
Red Tribe had missed it too, and he carved off a
piece of the very solid meat, and chewed on it for a
moment. Still good, a bit salty, but yes, Bixby could
handle this, and he nodded back and said, "Thanks
very much, uh—" and he stopped. He had no name
to use and the man smiled back.

"I'm Adams—Jon Adams—leader of the squad.
That's Kyle Stone over there with the black hair,
Randy Listers with the half-eaten mouthful, and
Sandy Alfonso to my right," he said, and all
nodded back.

Javor put the brick in one of the pots, added
water from his canteen to same, and stuck it at the
edge of the fireplace Sue was tending. She nodded
and got it a bit closer as she watched all the pots.

"We're Sue"—Javor pointed at their cook first
and then each one in turn—"and Wayne and Bruce
—I'm Javor," he finished off and smiled back.

All were grinning and eating, and even Bixby in
a few minutes too slurped and gnawed on the
pieces of deer meat Sue had wedged off the brick.

"Wish I had a beer now," Wayne said, and that
got grins all around the room.

As Sue ate, she asked the most obvious question.
"You guys are dressed like soldiers—seem to be
tactically capable, which means training—would
you mind giving us your backstory?" She scooped a

mouthful of what looked like some kind of chili into her mouth.

Jon put down his fork for a moment and wiped his mouth with a forearm. "We, yes, are trained—we're from the Shorecroft Patrol forces—our own city army. Well, I can call it an army, but in fact there's less than a thousand of us," he admitted as he slid another spoonful of something into his mouth.

"Shorecroft—the city that lies over on the coast—about, say, three hundred or so miles east of Maxwell, where we're from?"

That got a nod from Jon as he continued to chew on his dinner.

"Then you should know that before we were taken by the Red Tribe—the night before, in fact—we were ambushed by some folks in robes, disciples, I believe, they called themselves of the Forest Empire, they said." She spat that out. Admitting they'd been taken by two different groups in less than twenty-four hours was not something that instilled confidence in one's abilities. She looked directly at Jon and smiled a bit. "Course, we're free today, aren't we?" she said and everyone chuckled.

"Do I take it, then, that as you have Khuno with you—you found him with his K9 owner too? Khuno was his name before ..." he asked, but Javor could tell that this was a loaded question.

But Sue nodded. "We dug this one"—she pointed at Javor—"out of a zombie trap pit—and he tucked Bixby under an arm and saved the dog too. But no owner was there—in fact, we found someone dressed in the same jungle camo uniform further along in the city—he'd been shot by someone. But we did save his backpack—which no, we don't have anymore, as the disciples took it and that tablet too."

Jon nodded as he finished his dinner and slid the plate onto the wood-planked floor beside him. "Yes, there's a tracking feature on all of our patrol tablets —we lost ours to the Red Tribe too, and they just broke them right in front of us. We were biding our time, waiting to find a way to gain our freedom—so we're obliged to you at the least," he said, and he bowed his head to her for a second.

"Good shooting too, Javor," he added, and that got a smile too.

Sue smiled as well and said, "So tomorrow by lunchtime, we'll be in Arlington—love to present you to the leaders of the Regime too, if that'd do?"

Jon didn't even glance at the rest of his squad but said right away, "Aye, Sue, that'd work for us— we've lots to ask and to tell too," and he grinned back at her.

Undoubtedly, Javor thought, a new ally on Bones

is always a good thing …


#####

The walk into Arlington was uneventful, though they all took tactical positions for the last fifteen miles. By just past lunchtime, the sign off to the right side of the road read Arlington—and it looked like it was brand new too. No target practice on it, Javor thought, and that made him smile. Pride of one's community was something that didn't—or couldn't—come too soon, as there were other bigger fish to fry at first. But in eight or so years, someone had decided the city needed a brand new sign—a welcome to the city that said we're up and we're alive and we're well.

And below the name of the city was the icon they had seen a few times before—the red arrow with the gold star in front of it. Home of the Regime, it meant, Javor supposed.

Just past the sign, from a gas station on the right-hand side, four men came out to stop them. Each was armed with a rifle but not one was raised. As the leader got close to Sue who was on point with Jon, the leader of the Shorecroft Patrol group, he stopped and grinned, hands on his hips.

"Sue—is that you, girl," he said, and he bounded up and gave her a hug.

She grinned as he twirled her about a couple of

times, and she said laughingly, "Dale, Dale … yup, it's me—now put me down," and he did just that with a big grin on his face.

"Been, what, like a couple of years since you got sent out—you need to visit more—we've got some beers to drink tonight, lads," he said and beamed at all of them.

"Dale—my group here," she said as she half-turned to point, "is Bruce and Wayne and Javor. This is Jon Adams and his own threesome of Shorecroft Patrol soldiers—fellows, this is Dale Wilson. Was a squad leader back in the day—now, I see no insignia at all?"

He nodded at her as he took the time to shake every single man's hand. "Not used by city guard duties, orders from the big muckety-mucks. But yeah, I'm a sergeant is all. Good to meet you all," he said and then stepped back.

He and the rest of the group were wearing plain black uniforms of pants and shirts. No insignia of rank was visible either as Dale had said. Standard-looking boots, armor vests, and utility belts like those that most modern infantrymen wore completed their outfits. The rifles were all carbines, Javor noted, with big curved clips, which would hold a lot of rounds. No backpacks were in evidence, but as they lived here in Arlington, that was to be expected.

Each, however, did have an earpiece in one ear with the coiled cable tucked over top of the ear and then disappearing inside their vest. Javor wondered what that meant and whom they might be in touch with at any given time, and his answer was only moments away.

Dale's head was tilted toward the ear that held the earpiece, and a moment later, he nodded and said, "Aye, Sir. STAT!"

He grinned at them. "Technology," he said as he pointed at his earpiece, "means that they know you're here and they want to see you—all of you." He gestured to include the Shorecroft Patrol men too. "Anderson," he said, "please escort these guests to the Regime headquarters, STAT. No lollygagging either."

Dale grinned at Sue again. "Tonight, ask anyone for the location of the NCO mess on the base—first rounds are on me!" he said and clapped her on the back.

She almost fell over, as Dale was one big man, but she grinned back. "It's a date, Dale. And you'll buy more than the first round too—remember, it was me who took out that smart zombie at the picnic back then. You owe me ..." she said, and then she too turned and followed Anderson as he pointed down the street and into the city.

Arlington, Javor could see, was a city that was

alive and well after the Boathi had bombed it more than eight years ago. The streets were clean, there were citizens on the sidewalks, and even the occasional store was open too. He wondered where the goods came from and filed that away to ask about later, but on the whole, the city was so much more vibrant than anything he'd yet seen.

No cars or running vehicles, he noted, so the news about the Motor Pool would be of interest to the Regime.

As soon as he thought that, a sound came from ahead, down a side street, and a brace of horses, pulling a wagon with city folk, went through the intersection ahead. The horses plodded along, and the wagon driver waved at Anderson. The passengers were sitting on plain wooden bench seats, and there were even a couple of children there too. Bixby trotted over to a couple and sidled up to get petted and was a hit with everyone too.

He knew from his Gallipedia research that the Boathi virus bombs had wiped out the children first —yet these kids were not yet teenagers so that was a good sign, he thought. Of course, it was so hard to tell the age of kids that they could well have been born after the bombs fell … he really had no idea. Still, good to see, for sure…

Farther down the street, a food market was out on the sidewalk, and they all passed by slowly, eying the various food items. There were tomatoes, but it was spring, so Javor thought of hothouses right away. Hothouses would explain the variety of other vegetables too. He recognized cucumbers, cabbage, and fresh beans of some type too. Alongside the rows of tables with those items were a few display coolers. He went right up to the coolers and saw fish, chickens, and a couple of other animal carcasses he didn't recognize available for sale too.

Large ice bins held cold drinks and some other vegetables he didn't recognize. He was no expert on the crops here on Bones, but the fact this store was open and selling products and at least a couple of dozen city citizens were shopping was a good thing.

"Nice to see commerce coming back," Sue said, and that got an amen from them all.

As they walked ahead, Anderson offered up a note for their attention. "One thing that we do—back where we met—is to steer zombies away. We have none in Arlington at all anymore. That's a good thing—especially if you're trying to raise a family here too …"

With a chorus of amen, they continued walking. The city was big. The street they were on seemed to stretch out in the distance for miles ahead, and just when Javor thought that they may have to camp out before they got to this headquarters, Anderson, their guide, turned off on a side street to the right.

On the right of the side street was a simple park with a children's playground that was unused at the moment. There was a fountain too, but no water sprayed out of it, and it did need a new coat of paint, he thought.

On the left was an enormous building—one with the old-fashioned columns and steps that were a hundred yards wide. Only five stories tall, it was imposing to say the least. The huge engraved name of the building was way up top, and while he could see it, it was in a language Javor didn't know, so he pointed it out to Anderson.

"Where we're going—Regime headquarters. Hundreds of years old this building is, and that says Armories in a language that's been, what, dead for a millennia or so. We use it as it has all that we need—including, of course, direct in power as well."

As he talked, the group went up the long set of stairs, between two of the columns, and then past the pair of guards on picket duty, who challenged Anderson and got the proper response.

Inside the main lobby area, it was a hubbub of office-like action. Everyone appeared to be in the same kind of uniform as Anderson, but all had insignias showing—mostly of corporals and sergeants, Javor noted. A couple of times an officer with two bars went by, but he noted no saluting at all.

As they made their way by most of the people, they got to the escalator in the corner of the large lobby, and while it was turned off, they used it like stairs and went up to the second floor, turned to their right, and went up again and again until they reached the fifth floor.

There, Anderson led the way down a long hallway of what was beautiful woodwork, milled and carpentered to be visually impressive. Shelves every so often held photos of officers, companies, inspections, and the like. Old photos of old days gone by, Javor thought, and he noted the hallway was as impressive as it was supposed to be.

At the large doorway at the end of the hall, a corporal was on picket duty. The corporal and Anderson exchanged challenges and answers, and he grinned and opened the door. Bixby walked in first and that got a smile from him too.

As Anderson stood to one side, he said, "Please enter, take a seat, and the Circle—that's the bigwigs of the Regime—will be right with you ..."

#####

Maeve came into the room first, staring at the ones across the table and wearing what could be described as a sad-looking face. *Woman,* Javor thought, *of about forty-plus years, plain looking with no makeup or hair treatment, in camo that was too baggy, and no insignia showing either.* But his study of her was interrupted by the entry of six more members of this Circle—three men and three more women.

One of the women came around the long table to introduce herself to each of them. "Vera—I'm the leader of the Circle—"

"This year, mind you," Maeve interrupted.

Vera nodded and half-smiled before continuing. "As I said, leader for this year of the Circle. Our topmost body of governance for the Regime. And you are …" she prompted, and that got her the names and affiliations of everyone at the table.

As she was doing that, Finn had made sure that each person in the room got something to drink and a muffin or one of those delightful new cupcakes that had appeared this morning in their catering dollies. Why there were cupcakes was beyond him, but he did note there was a flyer there announcing the opening of another new bakery in Arlington— Cake & Loaf Bakery. Nice, he thought, as he bit down on the edge of one, the chocolate buttercream icing a pleasure he'd not had in years. Fussing about, he got them all straightened out and then took his seat to the right of Vera who was still instructing the newcomers with Regime history.

"And then, five years ago, once power and food

had been re-established, we began to think about us
—the people of Ceti4 or Bones, as we now all call it.
Our planet survived, and some of us citizens
survived, but our society did not. Further is the
issue of the zombies we have—both dumb and
smart. Plus there's the fracture of what we call
normal versus oddballs or religious zealots that we
just don't understand," she said as she took a
moment to take a big bite out of the cupcake that
Finn had put on her plate too.

She smiled broadly and said, "Ahh ... red velvet
—any idea how long it's been since I've had that
cream cheese icing ..." and all realized it was a
question not requiring an answer.

"Can you expand on that religious item a bit?"
Jon asked as he worked on making his second big
maple pecan cupcake disappear.

Vera nodded, but Nixon, one of the men at the
table, took over. "Religious groups—like these
Forest Empire ones—are hard to understand, at
least to us. The Boathi virus spared them, they
found each other, and somehow they believe that it
was not the Boathi that did this to Bones, but that it
was a god. They all drank the same kook-aid, as
they've turned themselves into a communal group
of men, women, and children who worship this god
—and hate and despise and, yes, kill or enslave
everyone else who is not of the same faith. Disciples

indeed—yet they send out squads to capture non-believers they call us to turn them into slaves. We hear that they're building some pyramids way up in the northern forests that will let them get closer to their god—no matter what the cost is in these slaves' lives we hear." He shook his head and went back to his cupcake.

Vera smiled and said matter-of-factly, "Anyone can do what they want here on Bones—but when it comes to slavery and death to non-believers, we feel that the Regime must intervene. Somehow. In some way. But permanently if possible," she finished, using a moistened finger to dab up all the cupcake crumbs on her plate.

She looked at Sue first. "Your report I know we'll get later—but can you re-cap what you found on your trip here, Sue?"

"Mostly the same as on my trip out to Maxwell two years ago—but not quite. We found a huge group of working vehicles hidden in the Motor Pool at the army base in Walkerville. We took one of those trucks and it ran fine—'til a spike belt took out our tires about forty miles south of here. Met some of those disciples too—they came in the night, captured us all, but were not really looking for slaves.

"They wanted a tablet that we found in Maxwell, and they knew we had it, and they knew where we were. Sounds like some kind of loran or radar at work, in my mind, but yes, they got the tablet. Jon here, from the Shorecroft Patrol, can probably speak to that on his own later," she added and the last of her cupcake disappeared too.

After more discussion from Jon and the fact that all their tablets were networked, the general consensus was that while the Forest Empire might have been a cult, they had some real technology strengths too. Something, Javor made a note, that he should remember too. He took the last bite of his cupcake, looked around, and then whistled quietly as Bixby stood up from the far corner and came over to accept his treat.

"Javor—you're our spaceman. Tell us, please, about your ship and its current abilities, if you would," Finn asked, knowing that it was time to get that out on the table too.

Jon turned and said, "Spaceman?"

Javor sighed and slowly took them all through the last few days aboard the Drake, the crash landing over in Maxwell, his sole survivorship, and the AI diagnostics that said the Drake would never go to space again. He was sad about that, but he held back that he had hoped that the pilot who'd switched on the AI remotes to save the ship had also sent out an SOS for the human empire to eventually receive and then come after the Drake. It really wasn't something to count on, he knew, but still a good thing to hope for.

He held out his hands. "I'm a new citizen of Bones, I'd suspect, and I will help all I can—well, help to get society back on an even keel, that is. Bixby," he said as he pointed at the dog still licking his chops making sure he got all the chocolate icing, "is my new friend, but he is really from the Shorecroft Patrol. Found him and rescued him—his master had been killed much earlier than I got to him."

Finn nodded, made a note on his tablet, and saw that Maeve was still typing up almost everything that was being said.

"We are always looking for good men," Jon said. "So if you're thinking about a place to call home here on Bones, Shorecroft and the patrol would love to have you," he offered.

That took Javor by surprise and Maeve interrupted that line of discussion right away. "Not interested, I think, in bidding for Javor and the Drake, but the Regime has other fish to fry, young man," she said, and even Javor felt the slight slap in her tone.

Before Javor could say squat, Finn said it for him. "I don't think that our spaceman needs to do anything at this point. Vera, I'm sure, would like to talk to him—well, to most of you—about something else. We have had a mission on our to do list for almost a year and have not had the manpower or skill to attempt it ..." he said, and he looked over at the head of the Circle.

Vera sipped her water. She looked around the table at the eight of them—nine if one counted Bixby—and she had a look of deep thought on her face.

She looked down at her plate, now bare of crumbs, nodded, and then looked up at them all. "I cannot speak for the Shorecroft Patrol nor your own HQ. But I can offer this. We think—we know —that we need to send a team up to the Forest Empire to find a solution to their growing threat to Bones itself. This solution could be purely diplomatic—if you can find a way to talk them into giving up slavery and staying within their northern borders that'd work well for us and the rest of Bones."

That alone got a snort from Maeve and a couple more at the table.

"Or maybe the solution might have to be that our team, umm ... goes to plan B and ends their leadership control on their citizens. If you think that should be done with a shotgun or a drop of poison in a glass of wine—so be it. If you think that you can get their population to rebel and revolt and, in doing so, change their reliance on slavery, then so be it too.

They all sat and digested that for a minute or two, and then Vera continued.

"I know that this is a big decision—but we'd like for Sue to lead our own cadre including Javor, and we'd like for the four of you patrol soldiers to join us. I will let you HAM into Shorecroft Patrol HQ for talks and discussions and would gladly speak to anyone there about this joint venture. Makes sense, it does, I think, combining two of the biggest remaining seats of government together ..." she said.

She nodded at Bruce and Wayne and said, "I'd like to have a minute with Sue alone, but you can lead the rest of your party out, fellows. Relax. Enjoy our city and you'll all get Regime credits to use too. Barracks is same place, Wayne—go over and take what you need, see Sergeant Reynolds at the quartermaster's building. Jon, you and your mates are also welcome to stay, to talk to your own HQ, and hopefully to join us too. Day after tomorrow, then."

After everyone except for Sue left, Vera stared straight at Sue and only half-smiled. "You need to understand first that the Forest Empire has enslaved or killed more than two hundred of our Regime citizens. They constantly raid us using surrogate tribes like the Red Tribe you ran into. We need them to disappear if we want to rebuild Bones —Ceti4, I mean. So while this part of your mission with the group is confidential—we trust only you to handle this, Sue, we wanted you to know upfront that it's a choice that only you can make.

"We will be arming you with one of our—one of our last remaining nukes, you can simply bomb their city out of existence. It is disguised, using our best technology, to look like a simple twelve-volt battery to power the radio that we've included. It will create a crater about a half mile across, so we want the loss of life to be kept to a minimum, please.

"This mission ending goal we don't like. This one, we know, will put a crater miles long in our northern forest, and yet that would be a symbol that could not be ignored for generations to come. We do not like this one—yet we know that you and the mission must have the ability to decide what is best.

"We hope diplomacy works and works quickly. Reports across our governed area are that more than forty more Regime citizens have just been taken into slavery in the past month. We need to end this Forest Empire's ability to hurt us and our own citizens," she said, and she looked directly into Sue's eyes.

There was no doubt that she meant what she said, and there was no doubt that Sue understood either.

Sue nodded. "I'm to make the decision myownself—I understand that—and I'm to keep the nuke on the down-low too. Still, quite a responsibility, Vera, and one that I will not waver from, you can trust me in that."

Vera nodded and then looked around the room at the rest of the Regime Circle—and there were only nods from them all.

"So be it," she said, rose, and then went over to the tray to take just one more red velvet cupcake. She left the room, followed by most of the members of the Circle.

# CHAPTER TWO

The pyramid sat, as it was planned to, on a full three acres of cleared forestland on the northern side of the city center block of land in the Forest Empire capital city. It was big, being more than one hundred feet per side, and the blocks that made up the structure were carved from pure granite from the shield.

The quarry in which the blocks were cut was only three miles away, yet the process of getting the stones each, weighing more than six tons and eight feet by four feet in size was the real work of the slaves.

Quarried from white shaded granite, those blocks were put up on sledges under which the rollers were placed and then pulled by the teams of slaves the full distance from the quarry to the pyramid building site. There, for the past year, the area to hold the pyramid had been ground down to the bedrock below to ensure that the new structure would be built level and balanced and maintain its preeminence in the Empire for generations to come.

The pyramid was an ongoing project for the Empire, and as such, it was the be-all and end-all for each of the ten thousand Empire citizens on a daily basis. Architects were in charge of the survey and alignment of the structure. Empire guards looked after the slaves, moved them from various locations, and set up the work details on a weekly basis. One week a slave might be toiling in the quarry splitting stone with wedges and sledgehammers, while the next week might find them pulling on ropes to slowly move a block of that white granite from the quarry to the city. Others looked after the final polishing and beveling of the stones once they were placed up the ramps and in their final positions.

The work of building the pyramid had been going on now for all of three years, and while that was more than a thousand days, the structure itself was now only forty feet tall. Each stone had to be cut to order, delivered on schedule, controlled and if necessary changed, transported up the pyramid flank on schedule, and laid down on schedule with its mates. Rope rolls were constructed using the finest steel that one could get on Bones, and with their mechanical advantage, the pyramid was slowly taking shape.

At the master builder station, located on the front of the pyramid facing, the head architect checked his plans yet again for the umpteenth time in the past hour. The stone that was slowly getting moved up the nearby ramp was perfectly cut and trimmed, and on its sledge, the stone was polished and burnished to take its place near the top. The team of slaves doing the heavy pulling and lifting to get the stone up that ramp was sweating in the morning sunshine. He could see their glistening backs from here.

By lunchtime, that stone would be in the proper location, and he would have his flagman wave the stone to stop. The sledge slaves would then unhook the stone from the sledge and lever it onto the side-beams. It would be moved into its final position for the stonemasons to finish it off. Small cracks and fissures often were the case after the stone had come all these miles, and the stonemasons were experts at getting every single stone to look perfect.

From where he stood, he looked to the west, down the long road that was now fairly level toward the quarry miles away. On the road, he could see the slaves who were slowly moving the next stone and the one after that one toward the city center and the pyramid where they'd lay. The average was now about five stones per day, and while he recognized that this was a real achievement to get that many stones placed in a workday, he knew the pyramid project was behind.

When he looked to his right, toward the floater yards, he could see there were only two at rest. Large black blimps floated in the air with their command, passenger, and cargo areas all contained within the shell itself. Each could carry more than thirty people with gear and even cargo to a small degree.

The floaters had been a find for them in the north, and they had once belonged to an exploration company that searched the north for ore deposits, oil, and gas. When the Boathi bombs had fallen, the bombs had not disabled the floaters as the floaters were powered by gasoline engines with propellers that drove the helium-filled blimps.

The Forest Empire had five floaters that still had to be taken up to the nearby oil exploration compound for fuel and helium top ups. The Empire used them sparingly; as a resource they knew was above all else the Empire had, they needed to be conserved. Three of the blimp technicians were now members of the Forest Empire, so they'd gained their own built-in maintenance crew too.

He had heard about other assets that were

warehoused at the oil exploration compound, but as yet that was only rumor. He would need to send up a team to confirm that discovery, perhaps with the next fuel trip.

What was still more important was the pyramid project, and it was to be completed in a little over a year on the fall equinox day. That day was special to the Forest Empire society as it was on that day that god had chosen to wipe out the non-believers on Ceti4. Bombs had fallen, it was said, all across the planet, and billions had died—except here in the Forest Empire. Here, the architect knew, they found themselves suddenly alone—and on their knees praying to god to save them—and he did just that.

It had taken almost a year for all of the Empire to concentrate themselves here in Empire City; even now, years later, sometimes new citizens came out of the forests to seek asylum and refuge. And they were accepted, of course, if they passed the Inquisition Board.

He smiled at that as some, of course, did not pass —they were non-believers who decried even the existence of god and claimed that he had not called for extinction of non-believers but that it was aliens who'd done this to Ceti4.

He shook his head. *Such non-believers were immediately found wanting by the Inquisition Board and placed into slavery to help build the new pyramid.*

They needed more slaves—labor to help move more stones and get the pyramid completed on its due date, only fifteen months away. He watched as one of the handlers had to discipline a slave almost right in front of him, the slave getting a crack on his shoulder by the handler's cane. The cane was hardwood, and when handled right, it left a serious set of bruises, and if it hit a bone with little flesh padding, it could break a slave's arm. But the handlers knew, like they all knew, slaves were not to be disciplined so badly as to make them unusable —so most of the blows were to areas that were padded.

*We need more slaves, else the pyramid will not be finished,* the master architect thought, as he once again checked the wide plans that lay on the builder's desk in front of him. Under the gazebo tarp over his head, the sun shaded out, it was almost pleasant enough to just sit and watch and wish for more speed. But more speed meant more labor, and that was not his area.

At the next project meeting, the architect thought, I'll have to speak up about the Equinox Games and the dozens of slaves who are sacrificed then. God knows, he thought, that we love him without the shedding of blood—but that, he knew, was heresy here in the Forest Empire. Sacrifices had to be made at the Games, to prove our worth was the mantra. He shrugged.

*Just hope that in three months and a bit we have many more slaves to help with the pyramid too ...*

#####

The *Sophon* sat off the last of their search planets, and the crew was stumped.

Not a single world within those twenty light years had yielded the missing human ship. They'd looked for nuclear power on all the search planets, and there was not a single bit of evidence found to indicate a human ship. The audit of these few planets was an extra for them, and they'd relayed their findings to the Boathi home world by Ansible. The audit showed that humans could come back from the bombing of a planet better than other races had. Perhaps, the captain thought, I should mention that to HQ and try to get the virus to be even more virulent.

He scratched his left ear opening, the dewclaw on his right forearm digging into the hole, and the sound for him was doubly loud in his quarters. Sitting at the side table, looking out at the last planet they'd just left without finding a human ship, he wondered if there might be something else the Boathi did not know.

How could a ship—a nuclear-powered ship—that

should be easily located on a planet with no other nuclear devices up and running not be found? How indeed, he wondered.

He smoothed out the sheaf of papers in front of him and then spread them out but found that too confusing. Instead, he spoke to the ship's AI, and eventually on screen in front of him, the view changed from the planet below to a graphic representation of the immediate area of space.

He enlarged the scale to show where they'd originally met the human ship. He narrowed the scope of the presumed twenty light years to show all the planets that the humans could have reached. There were only seven.

Each one, he noted, as he zoomed in on them one by one, had been scanned from low orbits for nuclear power.

Each one had come up blank—there was no nuclear power on any of them.

New settlements, new power sources, and new civilization and society on a couple—but no nuclear power.

Without nuclear power, no human ship could fly.

Therefore, there were no human ships on those worlds.

That kind of reasoning was infallible.

Truth with certainty.

He shook his head at that and the odd thought

that maybe the human ship had crashed into the sea on one of the planets and gone all the way to the bottom, thousands of feet of water above it.

But that too made him shrug. The scans the Boathi performed would find a nuclear reactor under mountains of rock or water. So the nuclear engines had to be found—unless maybe they were turned off.

That thought made him sit up a bit straighter in his chair and re-think that idea.

Why would someone, a human, mind you, so there was really no way of knowing, turn off their reactor? Yank the rods out of the fissionable material chambers and dampen down the whole reactor. Completely turn it off.

But why? Only, of course, to prevent a chain reaction via shutting down the whole reactor and to save their lives.

"Or," he answered himself, "to simply turn off the reactor—to hide it."

This was an alien thought to him, he realized. Turning off a reactor meant no power at all, other than what might have been available from batteries, for a few months at best. If the *Sophon* turned off her reactor, she'd be falling onto the planet below in hours to crash horribly. If the ship landed first and then turned off the reactor ... that might be something that a human might have thought to do.

But it'd been almost two months now since the human ship had fled. With traveling time and then reactor shutdown time, she was most likely out of battery life. Or soon would be.

In the very unlikely event that the humans would power up their nuclear reactor once again, he had to come up with something to help him find out when that happened and on what planet.

He spoke to AI again and then called in the Boathi chief engineer. Together they worked on a new addition to a simple satellite to be sent to all the planets they'd just searched.

Each satellite would be delivered by a probe, anchored in low orbit, and then monitor for nuclear reactor presence on the planet itself once per day. If it found same, it would send back word on that to Boathi HQ —and to him and the *Sophon* too.

If we've missed them because these humans are still hiding, like cowards, then we will find them once they think that they're safe …

Find them and then finally take care of them once and for all …

##### 

Javor sat in the sidewalk café with Bruce, Wayne, and Jon and smiled. Their table for four was at the apex of the outside patio, and it was closer to the big square in the center of Arlington than any other table. While he had no idea why, many items that favored the visiting tourist were in the square itself. Were things so much better that now there were entrepreneurs who worked the visiting tourist type of sales?

There were racks of large easels holding photos of Arlington—both before and after the bombs fell. There were photos of beaches, bridges, and even the Adair Dam too. Each of these photos was similar in size to what was once known as a postcard, as well as having the back side separated into both an area to write a message as well as an address.

All we need, he thought, not knowing if there really was one, is a mail system that a tourist could use.

He smiled and noted there were several street entertainers too. Some played an instrument, and he recognized a guitar of some odd type with nine strings; the instrument was played by vibrating varying sizes of metal strips over a central cored gourd. There were keyboards and even an old bugler too. When all the buskers were playing their own tunes at once, it was a wave of music that he was glad was distant from their café table.

One entertainer, a very old man, held Javor's interest. The old man escaped some kind of manacles that the tourists attached to him.

"Good trick to know," Wayne said, and everyone around the table nodded.

Javor sipped his beer slowly and savored the bitter hops that had been used.

Jon said, "Is this pretty normal for the city? This kind of tourist-type visitors?"

No one knew and the question remained unanswered.

"Anyone as yet got an answer for the Circle? We going north?" Bruce asked, and the conversation began.

"Far as we—the Shorecroft Patrol is concerned, my HQ left it up to me to decide—and we're going. You guys?" he asked.

Javor sat back to see what the cadre from Maxwell would say. Bruce and Wayne looked at each other and grinned.

"We're both in—Sue too. That's seven of us so far …" Bruce said, and the three of them looked at Javor.

He stared back. He said nothing for a moment as he sipped again from his beer. "I'm in too— learning about Bones is going to be easiest by actually seeing as much of her as I can see."

"Figuring," Bruce said as he tilted his head to one side, "that when the Cavalry arrives, you'll go back out into space, and the knowledge you've picked up here will help in the war. Do I have that right?" he ventured.

Javor smiled and nodded. "My round—if these credits from the Circle will work," he answered.

Jon nodded. "Was up first thing this morning and went out to get some coffees, and yup, they work fine," he said and grinned as he finished the last slurp of his beer.

They sat for another couple of hours, drinking beer with no zombies coming at them or tribes of slavers searching for them.

"Besides," Javor said, "I owe that big palooka of a disciple a little payback," and that got him a smile, and he toasted Arlington with the rest of the group.

#####

*The meeting with the Circle had gone well, except for one small point,* Javor thought, as he followed the sergeant down the third flight of stairs into the sub-basement of the big Regime Armories building.

*Vera had said calmly that she thought that Sue, acting for the Regime, would be able to get the job done diplomatically. Vera believed Sue was an excellent person to have at the lead of the group to get the Forest Empire to quit their ways of buying slaves and raiding the Regime's outlying towns via their surrogates, the tribes.*

*Diplomacy can work, but only if both sides have something to gain.*

The Regime would gain some respite from the Empire's changes in their slavery needs. And the Empire would gain ... what?

He had no idea, but he hoped that Sue carried with her some kind of deal sweetener that she'd roll out when the time came to help the deal come together.

Of course, there was the other way too—simply take out the Empire leaders and the population would follow a new course. One that ended the slavery issue.

Slaves. He shook his head as they all piled up while the sergeant keyed in some kind of code into the door ahead, and they walked into the armory.

He grinned. "Nice toys," he said to himself and went over to the shotgun racks to work his way through re-arming himself.

While he saw not a single manufacturer he recognized, he looked at the more than eight types of shotguns on display with backups stored in racks behind them.

He pulled down a shotgun and looked it over. Single barrel, pump action, looked like she'd hold about four shells, plus one in the chamber. He pumped the action a few times, and Bruce, who was nearby, looked over and shook his head.

"Nope, not for you. Move over three and that's the one you'd be wanting," he said and went back to look at the long sniper rifles in front of him.

Javor moved over and pulled down the shotgun in the fourth rack over, and it was a gem for sure.

*Lightweight, yet balanced. Single barrel, pump action, but would hold at least eight shells plus one in the chamber. Manufacturer was someone called Taylor Arms, which meant nothing to him,* but Bruce nodded as Javor hoisted it to his shoulder to sight down the barrel. *Not a combat shotgun, but still a weapon I could count on.*

He grinned at the sergeant and said, "I'm done," and tucked the gun under his arm.

The sergeant grunted and said, "Ammo?" He opened a drawer against the other side of the rack holding the guns.

Javor searched through and found what he was looking for—buckshot. He took more than five dozen of the 12-gauge double-aught shells with a narrow spread pattern. Great for alley cleaning, he thought, and he added a couple of dozen shells of birdshot in steel shot too. Good for dinner, too …

He found some ammo for his Colt and helped himself to a few hundred rounds. "Done," he said, and he watched as the seven others went through the armory and picked out their own weapons.

Once outfitted, they all met back up with the Circle in the lobby of the Armories, and their sendoff was complete.

Each carried their weapon and backpack. The Regime had also added new MREs for them too, and some of the flavors, he could tell, were going to be tough to swallow.

All packed up, they got pats on the back from Vera and the rest of the Circle, and then they were on their way.

Javor noted that each of them also got a full and complete set of maps. The detail was great and the scale not so much, but he, like he was sure everyone else had, folded the map to show the path north and west to the Forest Empire city, which was about three hundred miles away.

At, say, fifteen miles a day, that's like a twenty-day hike. Of course, it's a dense forest and there's gonna be rivers and maybe small mountains or canyons too ... but still. A twenty-day walk is not too bad.

He smiled at the Circle. He was sure this was going to be an easy mission.

"Easy-peasy," he said to himself as he hoisted his backpack and got her balanced on his hips and shoulders and walked away from the Armories, heading north and then west.

*Twenty days ... what could happen in twenty days ...*

# CHAPTER THREE

The path was not fresh nor well worn. Sue said, "It probably isn't much more than a path that deer take occasionally." Nevertheless, she led the way on point as the team moved always north.

The path curled occasionally around a dip or swale in the way. Once it doubled back on itself, and Sue left the path only to find it again just a few hundred yards ahead of them. Sometimes they passed by animals, and one time they scared a deer out of an area just off to the left. Hares jumped out of their way, and what Javor thought looked like grouse ruffled their feathers, and as they continued to advance, the birds took off and their wing beats could be heard for quite a while.

The forest that the path went through was about as dense as could be while still allowing the team to work their way through. Fir trees were in stands with deciduous trees interspersed around them. Often the path went between two firs and they all had to walk carefully as the branches would strip off items on their vests or belts or even crush down on their backpacks too.

Sometimes, the forest was so thick that the black spruce stands fell right down to the banks of the tiny creeks. When they came upon a small creek, they'd walk the creek bed itself—having wet feet was not as bad as not finding a way northward..

Jack pine, poplar, birch, larch, and hemlocks surrounded them, and all of them soared up to the canopy that was at least fifty feet above them. Needles covered the grounds in clumps in places and thinly spread in others. The brownish ground cover was also a problem as sometimes walking on it meant their feet got snagged in the calf-long strands, and both Jon and Wayne had taken a tumble due to their missteps.

Today, day two of the long hike to the Forest Empire, was a dull day. Whenever they could even see the sky through the heavy coniferous cover above, it was mostly cloudy gray skies. Javor had warmed up pretty early yesterday and had taken off his light camouflage jacket and tied it around his waist at lunchtime. Today, he started with the jacket already off. Being somewhat in shape and an ex-athlete helped quite a bit. But the reminder he was more than fifty years of age, and therefore not quite up to the level of fitness of most around him, was driven home whenever someone jumped over an obstacle and he had to go around same.

The path had petered out again, and Sue was now standing still, map and compass in hand, and she called a halt. "Looks like we're doing fine so far," she said as she pointed off over her left shoulder. "North is that way, and we'll stay on pace for the next couple of hours 'til lunch—everyone okay with that?" she asked, looking at Wayne.

He nodded and said, "Got three layers of them bandages on my big heel blister … it's still bugging me, but yeah, I'll clean and wash it up at lunchtime."

"Do not sit near me," Bruce said, "'cause today is MRE Sloppy Joes day." He grinned and that got a laugh at least from most of them.

Randi, one of the Shorecroft Patrollers, grinned and said, "Ooh … nice, blister puss for a topping," and everyone laughed heartily.

Sue traded off the point job with Javor who nodded and then took the compass from her and moved up to lead the team north. He pushed his way through the branches of a massive white spruce ahead and continued to push ahead north. Almost an hour later, he found a small creek wit the current coming toward them. He picked his way along the left bank, careful to watch where he stepped, and after about thirty feet, he saw something shiny in the creek near the bank.

"Hold it a sec," he said and tucked the compass away. He stepped into the water on a rock just below the surface and reached down against the up-current edge of that big rock. He grabbed the object and pulled it out of the creek, and it emptied itself of water as he held it up.

"Can ... can of oil it says on the side—and it's airplane oil. Least that's what the can says, and it had tables on the side showing vapor phase coking and elastomer compatibility test results too. I know a bit about this kind of item—and it's for an airplane engine," he said, turning the can over and over to empty it completely.

"Don't see any airplanes in the creek," Jon said.

Everyone was deep in thought and silent until Sue spoke up.

"Back on the hike, I'd say ..." she said.

Javor dropped the can back into the creek, and the current tossed it around and upside down as it went downstream and away from them. "New can though," he added as he took the lead once again and aimed them north.

More trees, what a surprise, he thought. Once again a stand of heavy white spruces lay ahead like a wall of needles they couldn't even see through. As he pushed through the branches, he stepped out and stopped. Behind him, Bruce bumped into him and called out, "Halt," and the ones behind him did just that.

Moving off to one side, Javor yelled back, "Come on through," and the rest of the mission team pushed through and stood in a clearing.

"A big clearing," Javor said to himself as he looked around. At least two hundred yards long by about a hundred yards wide, the clearing was just grass and weeds, which had been cut recently as he could see clods of cut stalks in piles near the edges of the clearing on one side. The creek they'd just passed by was on the far left side of the clearing, and they could hear it gurgling as the current moved down over the rocky course.

But close by, here at the southern edge of the clearing, there was a large set of four huge poles, each about a foot across stuck in the ground. Every ten feet or so, there were wooden connecting two-by-fours, locking the four poles together all the way up to the top of the poles about forty feet or so. From the top hung a huge braided set of ropes that had smaller connecting loops that ran all the way from the top to the bottom, like a ladder of some sort, meant to be climbable all thought. There was little else to see on this structure

Sue said, "This is like to hold something up—or down, I'd say?"

Jon nodded. "We had something similar back in Shorecroft that we used to hold satellite dishes—before the bombs, of course. You just climb up the tower, make any needed adjustments, and then climb back down."

That got more nods.

"But, who the hell uses satellites anymore," Wayne asked, and that got some shrugs.

Javor said, "But what is more interesting is that this area here—the whole area—has been recently trimmed. And wouldn't eight-plus years of normal forest growth have filled up this empty area much more than what we see? My point is that whatever this is—it's in use, I'd say."

Everyone contemplated Javor's observation for a few minutes.

Sue nodded and took a few photos of the area, and they all walked toward the far side of the clearing. About halfway across the clearing off on the right side, very close to the bubbling creek, were a large number of stumps and a large fire-pit too that still had burned remains of previous fires in the bottom. Someone had raided the creek for the stones that circled the fire-pit, and others had found some trees to cut to make seats out of stumps, which were placed all around the campfire pit.

"Someone used this recently—the rains of just a couple of days ago had washed the burned remains down in the fire-pit, I'd say," Javor noted.

They continued to walk on, and once they reached the far edge, Wayne took point and they moved off once again in single file through the dense boreal forest ... always heading north.

##### 

As the woman tilted her large plastic pot holding good drinkable water, the arrow went right through it and into her chest. She gasped and looked down at the arrow that had just pierced a lung and tried to call out, but she fell against the well pump in the middle of the small village and was hardly noticed.

Around her, kids played with toys as other moms were working on dinner inside their huts. Two men were standing guard and should have been more alert, but instead they were sitting on a log at the edge of the village, just chatting. As one of them reached down to pick up his canteen, an arrow ripped through the air and speared his canteen right into the ground.

Rising, he screamed, "Slavers," and in less than a minute, he and his guard friend were grabbed, hog-tied, and left on the ground. The attackers moved through the village, tying up almost everybody and letting some just run off.

Older women were of no value to them, so they were allowed to run away.

All the men, though there were few, were all tied up and kept.

Children had to be older, and most were not except for the two girls—twins it looked like to the slavers—with golden hair and young bodies. They were in the first flush of womanhood—a fact that was not lost to the slavers. The girls would fetch a very handsome price, and they gathered up all their captured villagers.

Thirteen men and the twins were shackled together in a string of chains, each having a wrist on the long chain that was immobile.

The slavers also went through the village huts and homes; they took whatever they might want or need. Food was important and they broke into the hanging lockers to take dried fish and elk as well.

They had learned not to burn down the villages they raided, as the returning villagers would then need to move their homes, and it was easier to attack a village if you knew where it was. Burned villages, therefore, were not in their plans, and they did take the time to put out the one or two small cooking fires they'd found in a few huts.

The slaver leader checked the chains; all the new captives were secure. He faced them all and said in a calm voice, "Do nothing to try to escape, and you will live. Do nothing to earn our interest, and you will live. In less than a week, we will meet up with disciples of the Forest Empire who will take over and transport you northwards where your futures lie. You are slaves as of now, get used to it—or die."

The twins were crying most of the way the first day they were force walked northward. One of the men, a skinny one who had some homemade tattoos on his arms, tried to jump away from the group when they were crossing a river. Two of the slavers held him down in the water until the thrashing stopped. One of them unhooked the lock around that man's wrist, and he floated face down with the current taking him downriver.

Every day, they hiked and didn't stop except for a break every three hours for about ten minutes or so. The captors were not mean nor for that matter did they go out of their way to hurt or embarrass or make their slaves' lives more uncomfortable. They were in the business of finding, capturing, and then transporting their slaves to the Forest Empire. Their job was as simple as that.

At the end of the ninth day, with almost a hundred miles behind them, the path ahead changed from a narrow path through the heavy pine forest and opened up in a very large clearing.

Ahead of them was something that got immediate attention from the slaves as they all looked over and up and up and up.

Moored to a large set of huge poles driven into the ground was a floater—an all-black blimp more than three hundred feet long. Where it was moored, against the large pole, a group of robed figures was climbing down the ladder there, and they walked over to greet the slavers and talk.

"Glad you're on time," one of the robed men said, and for a few minutes, they compared notes on the hike, the weather, the chance of rain coming later today, and more.

One of the robed men went down the chained line of slaves, taking a photo of each of them and making some notes on his tablet. After a half hour of cataloging the new slaves, he came back to join the rest. He handed the tablet to his leader and waited for him to digest the information about the new slaves.

The leader looked down at the tablet and then up at the man whose tablet he held. He shook his head and then went over to stand in front of the long line of the new slaves. He paid attention only to the twins—the two blonde girls who were going to be women in a very short time. He looked at them, and he went right up to each, touched their hair, slid a hand over their breasts, and grasped a hip on each of them. Then he smiled.

"We will be more than glad to accept this new

batch of slaves—and I can tell you that we will pay a full double rate for each of these young blonde women. Happily," he said, and then he handed the tablet back to his man.

There were some more conversations as some of the robed men slowly got the slaves unchained one by one, led them over to the ladder, and forced them up and into the floater. At the top of the ladder, they were manhandled by waiting robed figures who took them one by one to their lockups within the ship.

As the slavers turned and walked away, the last robed man on the ground looked up at the floater and smiled. The two beautiful women in his latest batch of bought slaves would mean the prime disciple would be a happy, happy leader with their addition to the autumn equinox chief sacrifices…

##### 

The white granite quarry lay a bit more than three miles from Empire City. Used now for hundreds of years before the Boathi bombs had fallen, now, it was used as much if not more. Three teams of slaves, each on their own shifts, days, afternoons, and nights, cut the white granite from the quarry, trying to hit their quotas. When the quotas were met, the slaves were fed. When the quotas were not met, there was pain and no meal at the end of the day.

Today was like any other day—well, afternoon really, Tina thought as she once again went down the same lineup of wedges all the way back to the first one on this block. "Blocks were split," she said to herself, using the same stupid voice as her shift foreman had used, "by driving wedges into the holes drilled to use by the splitters." That's what I am, a splitter, and I am good at it.

At least that's what made her speak up earlier about this block. It had an almost unseen line running parallel to the string of forty holes that now had those wedges inserted. It was her job to go from number one to number forty, tapping each with the same effort using her heavy steel hammer. Each went down only a small fraction of an inch each time it was struck.

Some blocks took about a hundred hammer blows, and others took more.

This one, she knew, would be much less, and she was right. On her thirty-seventh smack, the block split—but not down the perfectly straight line of the drilled holes and wedges. Instead, as she knew it would, the stone split on that fracture line, and the odd-shaped third of the stone slid off and fell to the ground. She stood up and put down the hammer on the remaining top of the ruined block. She blew the whistle around her neck to call over the foreman, and she stood still waiting for him to arrive.

Five minutes later, a disciple walked over and stood there looking. He studied the piece of the block that had sheared off and ruined the whole block. He looked at her and said, "How many?"

She answered, "Late thirties ..." and she could not meet his eyes.

"You're responsible, of course, no food today. You should also get five lashes," he said as he looked across the quarry at the Shieldsman standing there, "but I'll give you the benefit of the doubt—you did warn me about this a few hours ago. So instead of pain, you'll be training a new slave moving up from labor to becoming a splitter. They're to get the same training you did—and I want them ready to go on to their own blocks in three days.

"Now get those wedges working and split off the block—I'll see if I can find a way to cut it down to use it elsewhere. But I can't fix the numbers—your shift team is down one block. You'll have to make it up, no excuses ..." He turned to walk away.

Around Tina, there were hundreds of slaves, all working on the marking and cutting of blocks of white granite. Others moved then with those huge rollers over to the road that led back to Empire City and the new pyramid. The quarry was behind in the cutting and supply of the white granite stones to pike up on the pyramid to make it bigger and taller and, of course, to finish it.

#####

The prime disciple nodded to his chief acolyte and said, "Time. Find Disciple Anqas and send him in."

In the small audience room, things were much less formal than in the big public room. There, he had to sit on the only chair in the room, up on a dais, people requested an audience, and it was so formal. But it was necessary to show the citizens of the Empire how things were run at the top of the heap. He almost smiled at that as he sat around the circular table pushed over to one side of the room.

Until the new pyramid was complete and built as a structure, the chief builder had said he had no idea when the interior areas would be completed. That was where the new much bigger public audience room would be, and from his list of rooms to be built, he had also asked for a larger small audience room too.

Today, he had not even looked over at the stack of reports from the chief builder; well, that was a bit of a lie. He could see the stack, and it was about the usual twenty or thirty pages, but they'd say much the same thing as the ones yesterday had said. Not enough slaves to get the completed pyramid up and built by the autumn equinox for the Games.

He sighed.

*If there was one thing he'd grown tired of, it was the excuses of not enough slaves for the job to be done.*

He reached for his glass on the table and took a sip of the water. He only ever drank water, and there was always a pitcher of same nearby. It was water from the river at the side of the new pyramid, and he was proud to be one of the few in the Empire who really liked the water they had at their feet. He sipped. Cold … had to be cold … and still it could have been colder.

He motioned to an acolyte, who stood against the wall, and then pointed at the pitcher. The acolyte jumped to fetch new colder water.

"I am Disciple Anqas, Prime Disciple … I was summoned to meet with you…" the younger man said. Dressed in the traditional black robe of the disciple class of citizens, the man was thin, calm, and even servile to his prime disciple.

He nodded to the younger man and said, "Tell me once again about the seizure of that tablet … tell me everything you remember and you experienced …"

Anqas looked at him and tilted his head. "But Prime, my report covered all of that. Is there something that you want to know specifically?" he said.

The prime disciple looked at him and shook his head.

Angas continued. "What I can tell you is that we found them with the tablet that gave us their location as the Empire Network showed us where it was. We did see that it had moved about seventy miles or so, northeast in direction from where it had sat for over a month. That was the town of Maxwell. We used floater U-3 to get on our way once the tablet began to move, thinking that it perhaps was in danger of being read by someone who should not learn our secrets.

"We came upon the group that had it—they called themselves a cadre—and they were in the Regime—in Arlington, as we all know. We have had some dealings with them over the past four or five years, and we all know that this Regime is made up of non-believers. They will never prosper here on Ceti4 ..." he said, his voice taut.

"The Forest Empire and the Regime know each other," the prime disciple said to himself, and while there was no real hate between them, there was no love either. Each stayed in their own areas, and each ignored the other.

He looked back at Disciple Anqas and smiled. "And what else can you tell me? For instance, who was actually carrying the tablet—and when you asked for it, what did they say?"

Anqas nodded and said, "We found them during the nighttime, Prime. We quickly got their watch guard out of commission by putting a simple arrow into his arm. We also had to club one or two others, but they didn't put up much of a battle. We got the tablet—I believe Disciple Norq went with the woman who was the leader of this cadre into the truck that they were camping around under the interstate. She had the tablet in her bag, and it was in the truck. Most likely better sleeping than the bare ground. We got the tablet and it was easy to see that it was still locked behind the old owner's password security. I did check and it worked fine—easy to see too because the lights were on from the truck. We took their weapons—all of them—and then we left them. We did get them to swear that they would not follow us, and we did backtrack on our way to the floater to make sure that they kept their word. We raised ship and were back here in less than ten days, Prime."

He looked at Anqas and said, "Lights? The truck that they were camping beside had lights that lit up? Did that not make you think at all how is that possible?" he asked.

Disciple Anqas froze. He said nothing, but a moment later, he nodded. "Yes, I did not mention that in my report, Prime. I am sorry about that error—I never even thought that the lights meant anything. My report was in error, Prime ... I am so, so sorry, Prime." His voice was hoarse, low, and meek. He had made a mistake and the prime disciple had found that out.

"Do you wonder how I know about those lights, Anqas?" he said.

As Anqas nodded, the prime disciple answered, his voice loud and accusing. "Because your other disciples, all of them, said that the truck had its lights on—only your report failed to mention that. Is this the kind of attention to detail that I should come to expect from one of my disciple class mission team leaders? Is it, Anqas?"

Anqas shook his head violently from side to side. "Not ever, Prime Disciple—it was just a mistake for me to not mention that fact ... a mistake is all it was. It will never happen again, Prime—never!" he said forcefully. His face was white, and his eyes dilated wide open.

The prime disciple nodded and waved a hand at him. "This will not change your leadership of your team. You will, however, become a slave the next time that this happens, Anqas—do you hear me?"

Anqas nodded, nodded again, and nodded a third time. "Yes, Prime Disciple. That kind of mistake will never happen again. You have my word on that ..." he said.

He smiled back and then reached in front of him

for the special yellow paper mission orders and handed them to Anqas. "Read them at your leisure, but here's what you're charged with now. I want you to take floater U-3 again down to the same area as you were before. I want you and your team— I've added twelve more to that team, mind you—to look for where this cadre might have found that truck. A working truck would so much to help the Empire—and I charge you with the duty to find us just that. I understand that they must have found the vehicle somewhere between Maxwell and the spot you found them. Go back there. Search, search every village or town or hamlet and every building and every garage. Somewhere, there are trucks— and we need at least a couple of same," he said as he leaned forward.

"Should you actually find one or some—take at least three if they'll all fit into U-3. Throw out anything else that might block you taking that much cargo—even your team. Have them walk but fly the floater back here to Empire City soonest. Stay in touch—you have the means on the floater to radio us … so I'll want a daily report, Anqas. No excuses this time.

"I understand that being a slave is not a life choice many would make—ensure that you don't make me choose that for you either. Find the Empire some trucks, Anqas—as soon as possible,"

78

he said.

The younger man nodded and the nods never stopped as he backed away from his prime disciple and bowed three times as well on his way out.

The prime disciple reached for his water once again and thought that it was not cold enough—and he motioned to the closest acolyte to refill the pitcher, and the aide jumped as quickly as before...

# CHAPTER FOUR

The Shieldsman cracked the whip, and as the lashing end went out, almost the whole group of slaves flinched. The slave that received the whipped tip cried out, but not a one of them let up on pulling on the large ropes. This was the second stone of the day, and already, the whip had cracked a few times. Many, many more to come, Christian hoped. He didn't let up on the weight of the rope over his shoulder—he pulled like the rest of the forty slaves in his group.

Forty slaves made up one team, and there were four teams in each of the three hauling routes from the quarry to Empire City and the pyramid being built. In the past week, there had been some talk— gossip, he thought, about the addition of another team, but there had yet been no new slaves to populate that team. His sweat dripped down, as always from his bushy eyebrows, and the salty liquid made his eyes sting. He shook his head but did not let go of the rope, knowing that would attract the immediate attention of the Shieldsmen who policed their block moving along at the best speed possible.

Beside the route that he was on, there were two more, and each had their own slave teams and a block being moved. He almost snorted when he thought of having a race, block against block. Then he remembered that each of the teams had to move eight blocks in one day.

Rushing by him, every few minutes or so, the roller slaves carried the rolling logs from the back of the sledge that the block lay on up to the front of the sledge. Dropping them in place, they then turned to the back of the sledge to get the next roller log.

On the sledge itself, the white granite block was a carefully split stone building block, which was usually eight feet long by four feet square. It was tied always to the sledge, and then it ran on the sledge rails on top of the roller logs. There were usually two men too who had big long wooden pole levers to help restart the rolling of those rolling logs should the team have to stop. "That was the best job," Christian said to himself yet again, "one day it'll be mine," he convinced himself and continued to strain against the rope on his left shoulder.

In front of the sledge, the waterers very carefully dripped water on the sledge rails ahead of the rolling logs so the sledge would move easier. They often had to go and fill up their water skins and were expected to do that lickety-split.; That's not a job I'd ever want, he thought.

This was only block number two. With eight or more expected each day by each of the three hauling teams, several stones that would be placed in the pyramid were now parked by the pyramid. Each stone waited to be pulled up the ramp to their final resting place on the pyramid.

That job—harder, Christian thought, than my own—was going slower than the builders wanted. The whips flew much more on the ramp. Slaves who worked on the ramp could be seen easier than most, as they almost always had whip burns and scars, and some had, he'd noticed, scars over scars.

*Women too,* he said to himself, and that made him slough off the pull for a step or two. The watching Shieldsmen couldn't tell he wasn't pulling very easily, but that was only because Christian knew to walk just a hair quicker so the rope over his shoulder didn't go slack between him and the slave behind him. He'd learned this months ago, and it still worked, so he kept the subterfuge up for a minute or two more.

As this block was a casing block, it was one of the bigger ones to be placed at a lower level. He'd heard gossip among the slaves that they'd soon be transporting only five-foot-by-two-foot blocks — or so the story went. No one, of course, had ever built a pyramid before, so no one knew for sure. He slowed a bit at that thought and wondered if in all the slaves there wasn't an architect or an engineer who'd know.

The crack of the whip came second, as the tip burned into his right shoulder and he cried out in pain.

*Damn.* And he pulled even harder, and the rope ahead of him had slack but not behind him anymore.

*Damn.* The tip of the whip had cut him, and the blood dripped slowly off his shoulder down to his armpit and then blew away in the windy day.

About one more mile, he thought, to the pyramid, and he just wanted to get to that spot and turn over the block to the pyramid builders and their procedures of parking the stone and getting them all unhooked and then marched back to the quarry those three miles behind them.

*Only six more of these today,* he said to himself, and he just pulled.

An honest pull ... at least for a slave ...

#####

Kyle Stone, on point, noticed it first, and as he held up a silent hand, the whole group stopped in their tracks.

Being on point held a bit of a responsibility that involved security for the whole hiking team, so his call to stop and be quiet was met with instant obedience. In the bright sunlight that came down dappled between the big huge trees around them all, they stood still.

They had pushed on hard today and had made almost ten more miles since dawn.

He stared ahead, then turned, and said loud enough for them all to hear, "Move as close as possible to tree … and stay still."

The forest was quiet as all of the ears strained to hear anything at all. Yet there was nothing to hear. Normal sounds of wind, branches, and leaves rustling, yes. A small brook must have been close, and they could hear the bubbling of water faintly.

Kyle pointed directly ahead of them on their path. Something was coming toward them—but not on the ground.

Ahead, the sunlight could be seen in bright shafts of light as far as they could see ahead. But there was darkness too. A shadow moved toward them, a big dark shadow that blocked out the sun completely. The shadow appeared to be hundreds of feet long, and it was a solid black.

*Whatever it was,* Javor thought, *it was big, it was solid, and it was coming towards them.*

He hoisted his shotgun, took off the safety with a loud click, and took aim alongside the trunk of the poplar he leaned against.

The shadow never stopped.

It never slowed nor wavered.

It just came toward them.

As the front leading edge covered Kyle first, he sort of squatted down and yet looked up.

Nothing happened, and in moments, they were all swallowed up by the shadow.

And nothing still happened. The shadow drifted and slowly went over as they all looked up to see if anyone could determine what it was that was looking at them.

As the far end of the shadow came up and then the forest was back in sunlight, they left their protective trees and gathered in a loose circle to talk.

Sue looked at them and said, "Okay, any ideas what that just was that went over us?"

Bruce said, "No animal that big ever lived on Bones."

Sandy, one of the Shorecroft Patrol group, nodded. "Agreed. Not an animal on Bones has that size and can fly."

Jon added, "At least not in our experience …" and that got a nod or two as well.

Javor said, with a small degree of new-kid-on-the-block interest, "So then what was it—and more importantly, does anyone think that it saw us?"

That stumped them all. No one had an answer to that question.

Sue nodded and said, "I'll take point now—Jon and Sandy, on the rear, and the rest of you spread out—let's say about twenty yards between us all," and she turned to take the lead.

Javor walked and he wondered where Bixby had disappeared too—and he whistled. And whistled again and no Bixby.

That bothered him, and he knew that under the current circumstances, whistling was not such a good idea, so he gently called for his dog, but Bixby never came to him.

That bothered him even more, and he trooped along but watched the area around them.

In about an hour, Sue called for a break, and as they slowed down, Bixby came trotting out of the woods off to the left of them, went right over to Javor, and sat looking at him.

He looked fine, Javor thought as he took a quick audit of the dog. As he ran his hands over the dog, he didn't find a single cut, scrape, or wound.

He tucked a hand in his shoulder vest pocket,

and Bixby barked—a jerky bar lay there, as they both knew. But the dog didn't seem to be interested. Instead, he got up and moved away, back toward the woods off to their left. Like he wanted to lead them that way, Javor thought, and while it was out of their general north-northwest path, he figured it might be a short trip or a long one—but one that they should at least attempt.

He spoke to Sue, and she nodded, eventually, and once the break time was done, Bixby led off with Javor on point just behind him. The dog went along, between trees, around logs, over little rills, and even up and down a hill that they could have gone around easily, Javor noted. He was just about to think that maybe this was not such a good idea when he saw a row of alders ahead of him appeared to have a glade on the other side.

The group came upon a clearing similar to the one now more than twenty miles behind them. Same tower of poles, and same long clearing about twice as long as it was wide. Over on one side, there were again stumps—but more importantly, there was still smoke rising from the fire-pit. The fire had been drenched with water perhaps but had not gone out, and the smoke, while thin, rose above them as they all looked down on the pit.

Jon said, "Fresh fire. So whatever else we think, someone was just here …"

That got nods all around.

Bruce said, "And the question is, whoever was here with this fire—do they have anything to do with that shadow we just ran into?"

No nods now.

Bixby barked and Javor fished in his vest pocket for the jerky bar—and gave him all of it too.

"Don't know the answer to that one, but interestingly enough, Bixby found this one. Why or how, I've no idea, but for the rest of this march north, I'm going to be watching him a bit more closely. Good boy, Bixby," he said as he leaned down and ruffled the dog's ears.

"Good to know," Sue said, and she kicked some dirt onto the remaining embers and then stomped out the fire to put it out for good.

"Javor and Bixby—you've got point," she said as she handed the compass and map to him, "and I'll take the rear this time—let's go, one and all …"

##### 

The prime disciple, the head of the Disciple Apostles and the head of the Forest Empire, slapped his chief acolyte, and the man recoiled and fell on one hip. He slowly rose, gripping his side, and turned to face his leader one more time.

"Tell me again, Head Acolyte, why we might consider the delay of the next Autumn Games?" he said.

He knew the answer, of course, as the chief builder stood watching, transfixed, as he was the one bearing the bad news. His chief acolyte was only trying to help the builder by getting him to consider this before he got the news.

*An admirable trait, the protecting of the leader by his chief, but this had to be quelled at the earliest rearing of this kind of news, bad as it was going to be.*

He looked at the acolyte and noted the man was tongue-tied. He didn't know what to say nor for that matter how to even get out of the fix he found himself in. *Good. This is good,* and he didn't even have to turn his head to know that the whole audience room was quiet. Not a sound. Not a movement. Not a thing was done to draw his attention away from the acolyte.

So he turned to the chief builder and said, "Would you care to speak on this matter, Chief Builder?" before he went back up the dais stairs and sat in the only chair in the large room.

An audience was held daily, and he sat and listened to issues having something to do with the Forest Empire. And made decisions. And slaves. So his minions, who were here today, like always, were on their best behavior trying to make their reports.

The chief architect of the pyramid stepped forward and up one step to now stand on the dais itself, and his voice was soft and quiet, but it was all bad news. "Prime Disciple—it has fallen to me to report on the current state of our progress with the building of the new pyramid. The truth of the matter is, is that we cannot make the current deadline of the autumn equinox—with the current level of support, Prime Disciple." He stood still. He was more than arm's length away, so that was one thing. But then around the dais stood Shieldsmen guards, all with their spears at the ready should they be called to use them.

The prime disciple nodded and looked away. As he suspected, with a slave population of only about four thousand and some, they were just too thin, too lean, to get all the jobs done. Even finding qualified stonemasons to work on the finishing of each of the thousands of stones in the pyramid had been almost impossible, and he knew that teaching went on over every single stone too.

"We need more slaves," he said to himself as he waved the chief builder to step down and resume his place below the dais.

He stroked his cheek, thought for a minute or two, then waved over his chief acolyte, and made motions for him to take notes. "As of now—today— there will be new bounties established for new slaves. Notify each and every single slaver that we use—plus all the tribes that sell to us too—that we will double our bounty for new slaves. Strong young men will bring a triple bounty too. As well, should these tribes and slavers fail to bring in new slaves numbers-wise, we will then take them in as slaves. I want our pyramid up and built and ready for our Autumn Equinox Games, and I want no equivocation on that matter," he said to his acolyte.

He looked down at his chief builder and then half-smiled. "Chief Builder—you now have the authorization to go to our justice division and have them move each and every single prisoner doing time over to our slave gangs. From this day on, if someone breaks the social contract and gets found guilty and gets a prison sentence, they'll do their time hauling stones from the quarry to our pyramid. You are also hereby authorized to notify justice that there will be no time off for good behavior for anyone in your care. You are also authorized to add a new shift to all of your slave routes—we need more stones at the site. You will also notify the quarry supervisors to also add a new shift too," he said, and as he said it, the acolyte wrote it all down.

He was still in the same foul mood he'd been in all day. The daily report from Disciple Anqas, the team leader charged with the duty to go out and find the Empire trucks of any kind or shape, was still the same—again he'd reported no finds.

Later they'd be in the town of Walkerville and

he'd report on what that town held, and then again when they reached Adair. Perhaps one of those towns would bear fruit for the Empire. He shook his head and thought that perhaps he might have made a mistake in keeping Anqas as the mission team leader. He can always be a slave, he rationalized, and that made him feel a bit better. Not better than he'd felt when he'd sent back a message of FIND THE BLOODY TRUCKS NOW to Anqas—he hoped that'd work. He'd even given him full authority to fly the floater right out in the open. No need to hide them anymore, he reasoned.

He turned to the chief Shieldsman beside him. "Chief Shieldsman—you are also to hereby double your forces on the slaver groups. I want them whipped for the slightest of infractions to increase their efficiency. We want more stones quarried, transported, and then ramped into place," he said as he turned back to face the whole room once more.

He looked at them all and then spoke once more, banging his hand into the armrest of his chair with each word. "Is there anyone here who does not get what it is I want done?"

The room was dead silent.

The prime disciple smiled at them.

"Then go … and build the Empire our new

pyramid!" he said grandly.

##### 

As they walked on, the boreal forest was changing, but it was noticeable only in one way.

It was not as wet as it had been, perhaps, Wayne noted, and that made them all think for a moment.

The trees were once again mixed coniferous pines, spruces, and firs with stands of alder, poplar, and aspen too. *It'd been miles and miles since he'd seen a maple or even willows along a creek,* but Javor didn't think it was important to point that out.

*Trees changed. Not a biggie.* He walked in the middle of the group pretty much at ease and tired too. They'd already made at least twenty miles today—Sue on point meant there was only one rest stop in the morning and one at mid-afternoon. Now coming up toward dinnertime, the shadows were long and the ground, if it was drier, didn't much matter.

He had noticed one thing though—that there did appear to be a blaze on a tree every once in a while. It was a large dollop of white wood, where someone had axed out about a six-inch square of bark. There was nothing else there, he noted, as he took the time to walk up to the second one he found and take a good look at it. It was on a spruce, so the lower edge of the white wood where the bark had been axed off had resin clinging to it. Resin, his finger told him that was not soft anymore—it had hardened and he'd called it old blaze markings. He had no idea how old—maybe if he'd been able to ask Gallipedia he'd have found a way to determine exactly how much hardness meant how much time since the blaze had been cut. But there was no Gallipedia on Bones—but he did make a mental check-box to find that out. *Any explorer might need to know that type of information in the future.*

As he moved away from the tree, he analyzed the area they had been walking through. They had been following a path, and as it was narrow, he figured it was a deer path. It was only slightly worn, but with the drier ground, it was without tracks or any way to determine what, or who, had used it last.

Bixby was trotting along beside him, ahead of Bruce and Sue, with Wayne up on point and the four Shorecroft patrollers in the rear. The land was changing, it appeared, and yet the hike, the walk itself, was the same. One foot in front of the other, go around that tree, over that deadfall, and by that creek. It was boring but still almost mesmerizing really, he thought. Hike, hike, hike …

Ahead they could hear a river coming up, and of course, it was directly in their path. As Wayne stopped just beyond the tree line on the shore, they all filed up to stand beside him and look out over the waters. The river was almost a hundred feet across, and from where they stood, there were no eddies around any rocks or any visible shallows.

"Seems deep—deeper than a simple ford across," Sue said.

Jon pointed to their left, upstream. "Does sound like there's some kind of a falls or rapids up that way though," he said.

As Sue nodded, he took the point, and they followed the rocky shoreline to their left. After a few hundred yards and a curve to the right, a set of rapids fell about twenty feet with large sprays of white water and what looked like big V's in the waters.

"Chute, it's what they call these kinds of river formations," Jon said.

"And what they don't tell you is that such chutes can be very tricky to navigate if you're in a boat or canoe or kayak," Sandy added as they all stopped and looked upriver.

From where they stood, they could continue to travel the riverbank and then get above the chute, which appeared to be the only way across. Below the chute, the waters crashed on a few rocks jutting out of the bottom, but then the river was deep, so it'd be a prohibitive swimming attempt to get across with their full packs.

"Above is the only way," Sue said, and she led the way along the riverbank. As they passed directly beside the chute, all could see the water was moving quickly, and the sprays from those jutting rocks soaked them as they passed between the heavy tree cover and the water's edge.

Almost a hundred yards farther, the river looked crossable. There were flatter rocks jutting up and out of the bottom, and the river appeared to be slower. Sue stopped at a spot where the riverbank flared out toward the center, and she pointed at this spot.

"Here's where we cross—slowly. Foot after foot, feel for purchase, make sure that the rocks below are not covered with any kind of river moss or the like. Slow. Steady … and we'll all be dry soon after," she said, and to start them all off, she stepped into the waters up to her right knee. She rocked a little side to side and then lifted her left leg in and took a step farther into the dark river waters. This time, she was up to mid-thigh, but she shook her head as she was all right and then began to feel with her right foot to take the next step. As she did, Wayne followed her in, then Bruce, Jon, Sandy, and Kyle, and Randy went last.

Javor, however, had the Bixby issue, and he knew how to fix that problem. He used a short piece of rope to tie the dog to a tree and told Bixby to lie down. He'd be the last of the group to cross, and then he'd take off his pack, leave it and his shotgun on the other side, go back for the dog, and carry him over in his arms. It wasn't the best answer, but the river was far too fast moving to let the dog try to swim over on its own, he believed.

Step by step, Sue led the way, and as she approached the midpoint across the river, she had some troubles with placing her next step. "Deeper here," she said, and she took a step downstream instead, trying to go around the deeper hole straight ahead. She went five steps downstream and then tried to turn to her left again to go across, and it was still too deep. In line, the group continued to follow her, and she turned once more to head downstream.

After ten more steps, the water was now up to their waists, and the bottoms of all their backpacks were in the water. Each held their weapons above their heads, and the occasional spray of water from the jutting rocks soaked them.

Sue finally found purchase on the bottom, and the line of river crossers moved again toward the shore on the far side.

Sue, now up to her mid-chest, found a fast-moving spot where she could hoist herself up and climb onto a rock that was above the surface. Once on the rock, she shook off the excess water as best she could. The rock was only about five feet wide, and she was at the far edge stepping down when Wayne, who was next to try to hoist himself up on the rock, slipped on the footing and was gone.

His head went under so quickly, it was as if someone was pulling him down into the water, and the rest of the river crossers were frozen as he disappeared...

# CHAPTER FIVE

The *Sophon* still waited off the last planet it had searched. Each week, the reports came in from the seven satellites that had been sent by their probes to sit over the seven planets. Each satellite had one job —monitor for nuclear fission anywhere on the planet—as it made its low-orbit passes across the planet. Simple and easy and when a pass had been done, once a day, it sent its report to the *Sophon*. Each report was cataloged and then archived for storage.

The captain shook his head as he scratched his eyelid gently, his dewclaw delicately rasping against his green scaly skin with care. He sat and looked up at the view-screen on the bridge and wondered when a report would prove to be helpful. So far, every day, no matter how optimistic he felt, the seven reports showed nothing. Not a single case of nuclear fission had occurred on any of the planets their satellites circled.

He looked over at his sub-alternate and asked with a glance for that reptile's opinion.

His sub-alternate bowed his head gracefully and then spoke with the precision that meant he'd expected this kind of query and had an answer ready. "Captain—we do not even know if the humans would spontaneously turn off a ship's reactor—effectively taking away all their power. We do not know their battery technology either to help them still be able to run their ships. We do not also know if this is even possible with their technology.

"What we do know is that this theory is so far unproven as we have only had reports that say there is no nuclear fission occurring on these seven planets. Over the past month and some. Perhaps a report tomorrow might be the one we are awaiting —perhaps not tomorrow but the next day, Captain. We just do not know yet," he said, and he sat very still, awaiting the captain's judgment of his opinions.

The captain rose and walked the bridge for a moment, first one way, then turning on his scaly heel, and then back to the other side. He nurtured his sub-alternate's opinion and thought of what he'd said. How it made sense. For the most part, the

Boathi lack of knowledge of the humans' technology was what mattered the most.

He returned to sit in his chair and said, "Thank you, Sub-alternate … solid reasoning, I'd say. Let's wait 'til tomorrow to see what those reports tell us —but I am getting tired of this search. If we do not find something by the end of this month, then I'll send in the report that we have failed to find the human ship.

"I wonder if you all know what that will mean for us—for you mostly. My crew is responsible to aid the mission in this case, of finding the humans. If you have any more ideas or opinions, or if you can come up with an alternate idea of how to find this ship on these seven worlds—then I'd suggest that you do just that. Expound and let us make the judgment of what might work for the *Sophon* … else, the report of our failure goes in …"

#####

Finn once more checked the room, and all was well. Tablet charging pads were at each of the seven spots around the table where the Circle would be seated. Each setting also had a nice printed Agenda in its place front and center. As well as those items, Finn had also placed a pad and a stylus for those who still liked to doodle during the meeting discussions—not that anyone here did that. He smiled at that thought and how well Nixon could draw … but then he looked around the room itself.

The room was new here in the armory building, as the old one had been needed for more schooling space for the children. But the new room, now that he'd had a whole week to work on it, was much better. Still on the same floor, but much closer to the back of the building, there was little exterior noise to affect their meetings. Smaller, but still big enough for their meetings.

He went over to the now real catering display and checked on their latest offerings.

Real milk—and heavens, real cream too—for their coffees or teas. There were pastries again, and a whole lineup of donuts too. There were three kinds of coffees and, by his quick count, more than a dozen types of teas.

"Everyone will be a happy camper today," he said to himself as he took a prune Danish, balanced it on the top of his mug of coffee, and made his way to his seat, just as Nixon and Reid came into the room. They looked around for a moment and then grinned over at him.

"Nice, Finn … you did good, lad," they said in unison and went over to see what they wanted.

As they pawed through the offerings, Gemma and Harper came in, and they joined the two men. The four of them looked at the teas and the pastries together.

Vera came in finishing a short conversation with Maeve, and the two of them stopped just inside the room's doorway.

"Finn, you have done terrifically, with such little time too," Vera said, and Maeve, unusual for her, gave him a simple thumbs-up sign.

Everyone got something to eat and drink and then took their seats in no special order around the round table. As Vera was the head of the Circle, the governing arm of the Regime, wherever she sat, the other members tended to sit in about the same order. Maeve always sat on her immediate left and Finn on the right. The rest didn't seem to care, and today it was as usual, as they chatted about the surprising great weather lately and the huge flocks of early summer cranes that had taken to Arlington. Many young had hatched and grown, and they too added some extra depth to the whole newness of the city.

Vera turned to Maeve and said, "Let's call this meeting to order, for the record," she said, and they buckled down to the Agenda and item number one.

*It was first, because it was the most important item on the whole Agenda,* Finn thought.

"Right, items number one are the reports—more than I think fourteen, we have here, that the Forest Empire is becoming more of a problem for us—for Bones I'd suggest too. Slaves. They must have a real need for slave labor because there are, in those combined reports, more than three hundred new slaves they've gotten in the past few weeks, it appears ..."

She said it with a very plain value in her voice that meant this whole topic was alien to her. She hated the topic itself—and the lack of any kind of respect in her voice when she spoke of the Empire was easy to hear.

Finn started to talk but was cut off by Harper who held out her hand to stop him.

"Finn—sorry, but I need to say this. Anyone fool enough to be caught by slavers or tribes and then sold to the Empire deserves what they get. Not a single slave, I'm sure, of the thousands that the Empire has right now had the brains nor the gumption to stick up for themselves. Defend themselves. Defend their families too. I do not see this as an issue for the Circle to even put on the Agenda," she said, and her voice was flat, succinct, and scorning of the Empire.

Some nodded. Some didn't.

Finn took the empty awkward silence to speak up. "Harper—in fact all here—you need to think on this. Slavers and tribes are driven to sell their captured captives for credits or barter or some such price. It's the fact that they are providing the slaves to the Empire that might be the weak link in the slavery chain—as I see it. If we can get to the slave suppliers—maybe that would help?" he asked.

He really had no idea how they could do that. But surely, if you end the supply, the slavery issue would go away. Maybe.

"Or," Vera said, "that's not something we can do —how could we prevent the suppliers—the slavers and the tribes—from going out to hunt for captives? Would we buy them at a higher price, for instance, to create a better return for these suppliers? Create a slave marketplace to outbid the Empire? Is that what you mean by that, Finn?" she asked.

It might work, he thought, but then he shook his head.

"No, not really, Vera. That's not what I meant … but it is one idea. How we'd even know what the Empire pays for a slave would be a starting point. Male? Female? Kids? The variations are large, the costs unknown and, for the most part, unworkable, I'd think."

Finn had no other suggestions to offer. They talked for over an hour on this, and the only thing they came up with was more intel was needed.

Maeve spoke finally and summed up the item. "We all agree—we will send a team to talk to some of the tribes we know for their positions on slavery. What the Empire might be paying; why the huge new needs for slaves; who might be the major or biggest suppliers ... I'll prepare a list, and we'll hopefully have a report back on this information for our next meeting," she said.

Vera didn't even call for a vote and said, "Carried. On to item number two?"

"Walkerville is next," Reid, who'd taken on the ownership of that item, said. "We have had a team down there now for a couple of days, and here's the skinny we've gotten so far. That there is a middling number of zombies there, all over the army base but really concentrated in the barracks areas. They appear, it seems, to be under the guidance of a small cadre of smart zombies also there too, so our cadre guesses that they've all been bitten by the smart ones. That's not usually a problem, but in this case, that many zombies who can use weapons, use English, and take direction and orders could be a problem.

"In any event, the team was able to gain access to the base Motor Pool and count the vehicles, and it's all in the report. They have not yet had the time to work out a plan to find out what's behind that sealed wall—but they will get back to us when they do. Before they do, I mean, so that we can vet the plan and authorize same. What we need to do, though, is to consider if we need to take those trucks—bring them here, I mean. Is that not what this is all for—we intend to seize the vehicles—

maybe a hundred of same?"

That got the discussions going, Finn noted, and there were pros and cons listed for that vehicle seizure. Eventually, Reid called a halt to the discussion and put it to a vote.

Everyone raised their hand as Reid called out, "For seizure—safety to be the ultimate factor under consideration?"

Not a hand was raised when he said, "No seizure at all."

Vera said, "Carried. On to item number three then," and they worked their way through the rest of the Agenda, *mostly small points that needed their simple rubber stamp on,* Finn thought.

Once done, most opted for another pastry and a refill on the drinks too.

He was happy that the Circle had at least found a way to try to get more intel on the slavery issue in front of them, but he also knew that if he could help find a way to curtail that whole process … that would be the best answer for Bones.

#####

When Wayne's head disappeared into the river, all of the crossers froze—but in moments, three of them dove into the water themselves, still wearing their big bulky backpacks, to try to save him.

Sandy, Bruce, and Javor floated quickly

downstream, and as they did, Sue called out to them.

"Go for the far shore, we'll cross and run downstream to help," she yelled as she waved the rest of them to follow her. She struggled to gain footing that was secure yet speedy, and they all made good time in the remaining twenty feet or so.

As Javor struggled to find a way to float downstream, stay buoyant in the stream, and find Wayne's head too, the effort was almost beyond him. His right shin hit a rock, and it felt like he'd been stabbed. His left arm he held behind him trying to steer his progress down the heavy current of the river, which seemed to work until he slid sideways around a large submerged rock, and it banged his elbow so hard he lost feeling in that arm. He knew that his shotgun was important, but he still used it like a pole to push off the upcoming rocks that appeared as he was tossed first left and then right. Jon was beside him for a few feet and he shouted to him "Wayne? You seen Wayne?" and got a no in return before the river parted them again. Bruce was in the lead, and he suddenly tried to swim even more against the current as he pointed over to the left and downriver.

Wayne had been tossed over a rock ahead, and he looked like he was trying to get on top of it but failing as they all got closer, and downriver they all plunged.

"There he is," Bruce called out and added, "Head to shore, Wayne ... head to shore," and then he too began to kick in the growing noise of the river.

They were closing in on the chute, Javor knew, as he kicked hard and harder still with his right foot. The alien tissue in his right knee helped immensely as he kicked and slowly gained on both Bruce and Wayne. Finding himself closer to Bruce, he grabbed the man's backpack and pushed him closer and closer to the riverbank. Ahead only a few feet, Wayne had somehow been able to take off his backpack, and he too pushed it now in front of him, kicking up a storm as he too was almost on the shore.

The three of them hit the rocky bottom of the river shoreline with only feet to spare from where the river dropped down into the chute, and they were all glad to grab rocks and shoreline undergrowth to clamber up on the land.

*Sandy?* Javor thought as he grabbed the roots of a riverbank tree and turned to look behind them.

No Sandy. Not a head could be seen upstream, and with a feeling of uh-oh, he turned to look downstream and into the chute. He searched from where they were all the way through the chute itself.

No Sandy. Neither a head nor a backpack was seen anywhere. Nothing at the top, in the chute, or at the bottom of the chute.

No Sandy.

Below the chute, there was much calmer water, but no Sandy bobbing there either.

He coughed up something and closed his eyes to spit whatever it was back into the river. He pushed on the bank and slowly crawled up the bank as the rest of the group arrived from upstream, and he helped them all get up the bank and away from the river.

He doffed his backpack, rolled over onto his back, and gasped for more air.

Sue eventually reached him too. "Javor? How you doing?"

He nodded to her that he was fine and pointed at Bruce and Wayne.

"They're fine ... all soaked and got scrapes and bangs. Sandy?" she said.

He pointed out at the river and said, "Out there somewhere," and his tone said it all.

Jon came over and knelt at his side. "Sandy? Did you see him go down the chute?" he asked, and all Javor could do was nod.

Jon stood and looked down the river, shading his eyes, and he turned his head as he searched the river from side to side as far as he could see. He turned to Sue and said, "Let's camp here tonight. I'm going to walk downstream for a mile or two … see you later." He hoisted his backpack, and he Kyle, and Randy all left and went downstream, past the chute, to search for Sandy.

The rest of the group sat for more than ten more minutes to get some strength back, and then Javor remembered Bixby.

He said to Sue, "I'm going across again for Bixby, can't leave my dog on that side. But I'm going well upstream, swim across, then swim with him back over to this side. Should end up just a bit upstream, I figure," he said, and before she could talk him out of it, he left his pack and shotgun and went upstream. He called to the dog when he got about even with Bixby and then went upstream another hundred yards to where a large willow grew over the edge of the riverbank.

Good enough, he thought.

Walking in, he quickly was over his head, and he swam with strong swimmer strokes over to his dog. He grinned as Bixby licked his face all over, and then they both walked back upstream to the willow. This time the water was a bit shallower, and he could walk a bit more into the water, holding the rope still attached to the dog, and they both swam across with some ease.

Walking down the riverbank, they joined the rest

of the group still waiting for the patrollers to return, but they couldn't even see them as the river below curved off to the left.

He dug the bag of dog kibble out of his pack to feed Bixby first. As the dog chewed, he looked at his MREs and chose the top one—he'd try the lasagna—and he yanked the cord on the side to mix the chemicals within the packaging to warm the contents. As he waited, he noted that the sky was clear, yet there was a ring around the moon already.

*I've forgotten what that means too,* he said to himself and then worried about getting too old to be an explorer anymore. *Most of the best,* he figured, *would know what that meant in respect to the weather. At the same time,* he thought *that he'd also heard about fishing and how a ring around the moon meant something to anglers too*—and then he just grinned at himself.

The patrollers returned in another hour, and the look on their faces said it all.

"Found him—seems a rock in the chute did the damage, and he drowned, it appeared to us," Jon said as he dropped his pack and sat heavily on a log nearby. "We found a place to bury him and did just that," he said, his voice cracking.

He made a small fire and watched as the pine and spruce branches they'd picked up, which still had plenty of resin, flared up at first. He had found an older log and had jumped a few times on branches to break some of the dead gray wood off, and when he added it to the fire, he watched it and tended it so that the fire was soon just the right size.

Javor let Bixby watch him as he ate the lasagna, cutting it into squares and slowly masticating it down. Not the best for sure, but then he remembered MREs were a modern convenience only. Not a single thing within the gray bag tasted good, he'd found … though a couple he almost liked. But they gave enough energy to the consumer to keep you alive and fighting.

He half-smiled once more, fished out the remaining piece of the pasta, and flipped it to Bixby.

"You know, there's a lot of folks who'd say that feeding your dog human food is a bad thing," Randy the patroller said. "In fact, there's folks that think that doing so will harm the dog—something to do with their diet maybe," he said.

"Good advice, but I didn't feed Bixby human food—just some MRE dreck," he said, and that got smiles and a chuckle around the fire.

Sue clapped her knee and said, "Good one, Javor!" and then they all were chuckling.

That had broken the somber mood around the fire a bit. Javor nodded and then tossed the now empty gray bag into the fire-pit. They relaxed and after a bit, Jon asked Sue about their progress.

She nodded and then fished into her pack and brought out her map. "From our distances over the past six days now at about fifteen miles a day, we're about ninety miles into the hike. Which would mean, if I can sort of figure that here on the map, we're about here ..." she said as she pointed to the solid green areas northwest of Arlington.

"So, if I'm correct, we're about one-third the way to the Forest Empire city—if I'm correct. I do note that there is another major river coming up, we've not yet gotten to it, and it looks like it's about halfway to the city. We should hit the river in about three or four days, I'm figuring," she said, and that made them all nod.

They finished their evening meal and watched the fire like most humans do. Sleep would come quickly tonight, and yet another river was the thing that kept some awake well past the time when the embers went out.

##### 

Anqas hadn't worried as much about a mission more than the one he was on right now. He barked at his team, he swore at the floater pilot, and he cursed at every big building or garage that they floated above. They landed, and the away team went into them all, one by one, and found no trucks.

For the first few days, they had tried to find keys

or a way to start some that were parked legally on
town streets, but if they were parked legally, the
owners had, of course, walked away with the keys.
They had also tried to find some trucks that were
out on the streets and had been in accidents when
the Boathi had bombed them, but they wouldn't
start at all.

Some had corpses still inside, long ago eaten by
scavengers and the like, empty corpses of blood and
flesh and even their souls were gone, he thought.
Non-believers always had a chance to come over to
the real God—his God. But seldom did they ever
see the light ...

He looked down in the floater's pilot area and
smiled.

While Maxwell had been a real disaster, perhaps
Walkerville, the next big town down the interstate,
might be a better spot. Maxwell had no large
institutions like an army base or even a regional jail
to look at, but they'd still scoured the whole town.
At every bridge across the river, every strip plaza
and mall, and every church lot and library, they'd
looked for a truck that would start. They'd tried
them all, every one of his team jumping up to look
into the cab, searching for keys, and in those few
cases they found keys, only two had even started.
Started was the word he used; however, they didn't
truly start. Those two had coughed, the starter

motor had turned the engine over and almost caught, but both never started. They moved on, taking the full week to clear Maxwell of a working truck.

He had thought to try the larger industrial parks, and they'd flown over some in the outskirts of the city. It was on one such a side trip that someone below had fired up at them a few times. He'd commanded the co-pilot to rain down a fusillade of their .50 caliber machine guns, and that took out a whole side of a three-story building below. He smiled at that, and then he had the gunner lay down a spread that would take out the next two buildings between the floater and the road. The resulting smoke and sounds felt good.

*No trucks so far, but we can knock down a building if we need to,* he thought.

They had run into zombies. Being up so high meant they hadn't attracted these flesh eaters, but he didn't think that fact mattered. Once, on one of the bridges, he was able to see that a pack of them had cornered a group of what looked like a family traveling together. They had an old mule pulling a cart with a woman, most likely the mom, doing the driving with some young kids in the back. A man, probably the dad, and a couple of older boys walked along. The small caliber rifle shots had attracted the floater over, and as they came up over the bridge just a few hundred feet up, only the family looked up in awe.

The zombies were not interested as they couldn't smell them up that high, but they were all stalking the family and jamming them up against the corner of the bridge and a bunch of cars piled together where the bridge met the street.

He motioned for the pilot to swing her around so that the zombies were right in front, and he had their gunner lay down a barrage to take out as many as he could. Of the dozens of zombies below, only ten or so fell, but that had given the surviving ones enough flesh to eat for now. He had the floater take a position up between the family and the remaining zombies until they were able to get their mule turned around. They took off quickly down the street alongside the river.

*We helped non-believers,* he said to himself. *That was a good thing. Too bad we don't have any kind of a flyer to toss over so that they'd know who just saved them and that we're always looking for new converts.*

Maxwell, on the whole though, had not been a good start to the mission.

Walkerville loomed on the horizon, and he had the pilot take the floater up to a few thousand feet so they'd get a good look at this small town and what lay below. In its prime, the town had probably held about ten thousand inhabitants. The first things they noticed were a single downtown main street and a few side streets with what looked like commercial buildings. It had been years since anyone sold anything here, so as they knew, those areas would most likely not hold any usable vehicles.

They thought the huge area off to the side that held the army base might hold fruit. He directed the pilot to take her down to about a thousand feet and float above the major road into the base.

As they did that, some figures came out of what appeared to be rows of barracks, and some pointed up at them.

"Zombies, I'd guess," the pilot said. And while he was right, there was something else to consider.

"We're too high to smell, the engines make little noise really, so what did we do that attracted their attention," he asked.

"Those ones," the co-pilot said, "are smart zombies. Notice the rifles over their shoulders?" he added.

That got immediate attention from them all. Smart zombies, unlike their dumb cousins, could talk, reason, and use weapons, and they kept up a semblance of a society too. While they were still flesh eaters, they didn't do the same blind stalking their dumb cousins did all the time. *That, and they were very, very few in number*, Anqas said to himself.

He motioned to float right over them and told the co-pilot to film this and record same to send back to Empire City too.

The floater gently wafted above the ten smart zombies, and they noted the group on the ground just followed the U-3 with their eyes at first, slowly turning as the floater went over. Down the road, they floated, still at a thousand feet, and eventually they reached the end of the barracks area and turned in a big curve to come up on the next major road back into the base.

"Let's look for trucks, it's why we're here," he said, and the floater crisscrossed the whole of the base slowly and methodically.

The co-pilot said, "Them smart zombies are still right there, just watching us is all they're doing," he said, and he was right. While it had taken almost a full twenty minutes to cover the base, the group had not moved.

"Let's look for buildings where they might have trucks inside," Anqas said.

The pilot nodded and went back up to the front of the base where it joined the town street. He turned the ship around there, and they once again went down the same street, but this time, he went down to only two hundred feet. "Coming up on the right," he said as he looked at the map pinned on the dash, "is their general admin building, besides

which is the Provost building—that's the army
police," he explained.

"Next on the left is a strip of smaller trailers—
dunno what they are 'cause the map doesn't even
have them on the base at all, and then on the right—
uh-oh."

As he said that and the eyes in the pilot's area all
turned to the right, an enormous building, the size
of many football fields, with the words Motor Pool
on it came up. A massive door had a pile of what
looked like broken-up wooden pallets in the
opening. There was an orange dumpster there too,
and while they were up at two hundred feet, one
could see there were at least a couple of trucks too.

"Bingo," Anqas said, and he added, "We need to
get into that building with no zombie intervention,
so maintain this height, and bear down on them.
Co-pilot, I want you and the gunner to take those
zombies out—every single one of them."

The floater continued to bear down on the rows
of barracks still ahead. As they got closer, barely
within range of the .50 caliber guns, he'd already
gotten ten of the team members ready to disembark
and to finish off what the big guns left behind.

"Time, co-pilot—clean the street, lad," he said,
and the thunderous tumult of those .50 caliber guns
opened up.

*The gunner outdid himself,* he thought, as those less

than a dozen smart zombies started to fall, from right to left. He watched as a couple of them tried to get their rifles off their backs, and they too fell as those huge rounds drove through them like a hot knife through butter. They fell like cord wood, and in less than half a minute, all were down.

He waved off the barrage and noted they weren't moving. He considered the smart zombie issue at the base as over.

"Fine, spin us around, pilot, and put her down right beside those broken-up pallets, please. Team members, looks like we shan't need your help with the zombie problem, but you're off the ship first. I want a full inspection of the whole Motor Pool interior. No surprises, shoot to kill, and watch out for zombies, of course," he said.

The floater spun, and in a few more minutes, the ship had settled upon the road pretty close to the building.

Those mission members were off right away, not even bothering with the ladders, and entered the building quickly, while the floater landing crew tied her down a few feet up and off the road.

They sat and waited, and he made sure the pilot had the rear-facing cameras on the pilot area view-screen so they could see behind them and down the road to where those zombie corpses now lay in the road.

He had to wait for five minutes, but then the away team leader came over to stand beside the side windows to report.

"Disciple Anqas—the building is secure. There are at least one hundred trucks in there—all kinds and sizes and styles. We noted both army ID on some and commercial food products signage on others. There are also what I know is called flats, I believe—they're trucks with low profiles that can carry heavy, heavy loads, Disciple."

"Fine, let's see if we can't get one of them to start, shall we?" he said, and as he did, from inside, the vroom, vroom of a truck starting up surprised them all. He grinned and said, "Let's go!"

It took only a minute to find a smiling team member sitting in a commercial food truck of about twelve feet in length that he'd just started. He grinned at them, and they grinned back. Anqas mimicked turning the truck off, and he did just that.

"Nicely done. Were the keys in the ignition?" he asked, and that got a nod.

Turning to the team members but then remembering the zombies, he stationed six of the team members to patrol the doorway and the floater, and to the other six, he gave instructions: find us bigger trucks—trucks that could be used to haul the huge stones from the Empire quarry to the pyramid, and off they went.

Around him stretching off for at least another hundred yards or so, there were all kinds of trucks parked in neat orderly rows. Probably more than a hundred of them, Anqas thought. Some were definitely army trucks, the dull green and camouflage tops easy to identify. Others were retail delivery trucks with smiling customers grinning from the side. Some advertised some kind of cookie, two thin black rings around a white icing center. Others had families in their cars, snacking on some kind of a chip and more too. Besides those trucks were even bigger trucks with eighteen wheels and plain tarps protecting whatever cargo they carried or had carried.

Around him in the Motor Pool, Anqas heard engines starting up. Some started right away, but some didn't start at all. As he stood there, he looked over at the big dollies interspersed with the trucks and wondered what purpose they served.

The dollies held big bins to carry something, and he strode over to look within one of those bins. The bin carried some of those retail food packs he'd not seen in years.

In about ten minutes, the six inside the Motor Pool came back, and each had something to offer. What he gathered was that almost all the trucks the group had tried to start had started—well, almost all of them.

One or two didn't start. But a dozen had started up fine. Of those dozen, five had been army trucks, more suited to carry soldiers in the back. Seven had been bigger and longer and could carry heavy loads, they'd figured. Float trucks someone had called them, but he didn't know what that meant.

He said, "Show me," and off they all walked.

Two of them were not right, he thought. They looked like they had some specialized kind of infrastructure on the decks of the back end to carry special equipment. He did try to see if such steel extras might be disassembled, but it didn't look like it to him. Three more looked right but were too short, he thought.

That left them with two prime candidates. Each was powered by a huge cab-over front end. The decks behind those drive units were wide and seemed to be just a flat bed of steel rails. Exactly the kind of thing we need to carry stones, he thought and grinned at the group.

"Bingo again and well done," he said, and then he handed off the job of getting those two trucks out of the Motor Pool building and out front.

He went back out to the floater and gave instructions to the pilot and co-pilot to move the floater to take on the two trucks, and he knew, after pacing off the length of those two, that they'd all fit just fine.

It took almost another hour to gently float the U-3 into a space where the huge rear doors could be lowered and then to drive on the two trucks. He was glad the support crew had been smart enough to bring along the needed tie-downs and stanchions to help firm up the trucks on the ship.

He watched as they worked. His number two came and asked if he wanted to walk down to look over the zombies. He didn't bother, but he did send a few of their armed mission members to do just that, and he asked them to gather anything they had and bring it back.

He also took a few minutes to go and get his tablet and take it into the floater's hold. He positioned himself in front of them both as he recorded his report about being successful and that they were on their way back to Empire City within an hour. He knew he couldn't sound smug, but he did thank the members of his team and the U-3 crew to the prime disciple.

They were loaded. All members were back on board the floater. The pilot said if they could get at least half of their top speed with the newly loaded trucks, they'd be home in about ten days.

He smiled. *God was good,* he thought. *Very, very good …*

FE-CreateSpace

# CHAPTER SIX

*Bixby was acting funny,* Javor thought. *Sometimes when he was spooked, he'd walk with stiff legs, like he was now, but it wasn't the same as before. Every once in a while, he'd look to the left, stiff-leg walk, and then be okay for a few hundred yards. He'd look to the right occasionally, do the same stiff-leg walk, and then let it pass.*

Javor had called a halt twice—he was on point—but each time he'd walked toward where Bixby was looking and found nothing. So they hiked once again.

If they could count on the general feeling of how far they had come based on the landmarks they'd met up with, according to the map, they were right on top of the Forest Empire city. But ahead was only more boreal forest, pines, spruces, and firs as

127

far as one could see. Not, Javor thought, that that was far. The trees here grew so close it was like trying to walk through a solid bank of trees.

They pushed through the heavier spruces with a forearm braced across their faces and gave enough room in between to allow the branches to snap back before the next hiker went through. Pines were easier as they grew taller and their branches all started above their heads. Firs were much like the pines, Javor noted, and that at least got him some relief, as it appeared they were now in a huge patch of firs.

Bixby trotted alongside him, no weird behaviors, so that too was good.

He thought that all was well and that since this morning, they'd covered at least ten more miles and lunch was long overdue.

He found a small pocket of dead firs with some blow-downs on the needle-covered red ground, and he called a halt.

It took almost a full minute for them all to catch up, and he said, "Lunch?" and that got nods.

Doffing his pack, he laid his shotgun down beside it and then dug in for the kibble for Bixby. He put a good healthy handful into a pile on the needles and looked for the dog. Bixby was nowhere to be found, and so he whistled.

Instead of the dog bounding out of the firs

around him, a dozen black-robed disciples stepped out of the firs, bows drawn on them all.

Javor said, "We've got company" as he slowly stood up and looked at the figures around him.

Sue and Bruce froze. Jon and his crew wheeled and went to pick up their arms. The bowmen stepped forward to warn them off. Wayne was still digging in his pack, and he said, "Company … what, we got bears here, do we?" When he finally looked up and saw the robed figures, his voice died away.

One of the robed figures, not carrying a bow that pointed an arrow at them, stepped out from behind the others and came to stand in front of Javor.

"I welcome you to the Forest Empire, and you must pardon our Shieldsmen who have you at a disadvantage," he said, and he gave a small bow to them all.

The man who spoke looked to be about six feet tall and had a slight beard indicating he'd not shaved today. He wore the same robe they all wore, and he had a medallion on his chest of a triangle over top of a circle in what looked like gold perhaps.

The one in charge, Javor thought, so he stepped forward to meet their captors, but Sue held him back and moved in front of him to speak for their group.

"I am Sue, and we are from the Regime—from Arlington, well south of here. We are seeking the city of the Forest Empire to discuss a matter of great importance with the prime disciple."

The black-robed leader nodded. He said, "Undraw," and the whole group of archers around him backed off their drawn arrows.

Things got a lot more civil, Javor thought, with that simple action.

"We can help you as we are one of the Shieldsmen teams charged with the duty to protect Empire City," he said as he pointed just off to the left, "which lies less than a mile in that direction."

How he could know that when there were no landmarks other than the green branches of the thick forest around them was a skill that would be a great one to have, Javor thought.

Sue smiled politely at the leader in his black robes and said, "Then let's get to the city as soon as possible so we can meet with the prime disciple." She half-turned to pick up her pack once more.

"For your own safety, we would need to disarm you, you would need to realize that," the leader said, and things once more got rather uncivil in the clearing in the firs.

Sue nodded, and slowly picking up her rifle by the barrel, she handed it to the closest archer to her. *She was careful,* Javor thought, *to move her pack out of the way,* though that made no sense to him.

The rest of the group then followed her lead, and while it took two of them to gather up and hold all the long guns, Javor noted he was still armed with his Colt. He assumed that others still had handguns in their control.

In a line, led by the leader of their captors, the entire group followed, and Javor noted that Bixby was back from wherever he'd gone. *Bixby was friendly with members of the Forest Empire,* it appeared, but had been trying earlier to let him know they were being tracked and followed too. *Good to know and remember,* he thought, and he mentally checked that box off too, like all good explorers would have. Not much of a human explorer anymore, but I'm determined to do better on a planetary scale. *At least try,* he thought.

The firs were still in the majority around them as they walked. They crossed a small brook that was only knee deep, but he noted it had some good size fish. He tried to kick one and almost got it, and one of the archers said, "Farmed trout ... we run the whole stream with caged entries and harvesting too," and he smiled at Javor. *Fellow angler,* he thought, and that made him feel like he wasn't so much of a captive.

After just a bit more than a mile, they came through a heavy patch of spruce, and the coniferous trees that had blocked them from seeing for many miles parted ahead. And there lay the Forest Empire city.

Small low buildings that looked like they were all built at the same time was the first thing that he saw. The buildings were in neat rows, all laid out in surveys, around the center of the city. Taller buildings were downtown, which were probably commercial in nature though he couldn't yet rule out some kind of industrial use too.

The main street led from just off to their right. In a perfect straight line, the road headed toward a pyramid being built. At the end of the main street, the pyramid lay in its shiny white glory. It was about four stories tall right now, he thought, and a ramp rotated around the whole structure. Even from here, he could see lines of slaves moving— pulling, it appeared—massive shaped blocks of more granite up those ramps. On one side, he saw what looked like a parking lot for stones that were quarried and not yet going up the ramp. And then he saw a truck.

It was coming down a small hill on the road, if it could be called that, and on it were six stones of great size. The truck was a cab-over, and behind it was a trailer that was only four feet above the road —a float trailer if he could count on his memory from years ago. Riding on the trailer, alongside the

132

stones, even sitting on some, was a whole pack of slaves too, whose job, he thought, might be the manhandling of those stones off the trailer when it reached the stone parking area.

The robed leader let them just stand and watch for a moment too. As they all stared, Sue pointed past the pyramid itself and said, "What is that structure?" and Javor thought that, like him, she'd been able to figure out most of what she saw too.

She was pointing at what looked like some kind of an outdoor stadium or arena. There were some bleachers made of wood being erected on both sides. Long straight rows of seating went up at least now as high as the unfinished pyramid. Seating, he thought as he'd been inside that kind of stadium many, many times over his decathlon career, which would hold at least six or seven thousand fans. The question was fans of what, and while that was not so important, he too wondered.

"That will be, when it's complete, our Equinox Games stadium. You can't really see it well from this far out of town, but it's where the Games will be run, where we give slaves the chance to escape. Or not," the leader said as he turned away from the group and led them all down and into Empire City. "Once we arrive, you will be allowed to rest and cleanup, of course, before your audience with the prime disciple at tonight's welcome dinner … so

I've been told ..."

#####

The smart zombie who was in charge of the base, Rita, leaned over and slapped her hand down on top of the pile of papers on the table. She obviously wanted to say something, but she just glared at the rest of them around the table.

Only ten days ago, there had been an event here on the Walkerville Army Base that had been poorly handled, and she wanted the guilty ones to step forward and admit that they had made a mess of an opportunity. But not one at the table spoke up, and her hand slapping the table only made them jerk up a bit in their chairs.

"Okay, let's see if I can re-cap where we are—and who's to blame here. About ten days ago, a blimp of some kind, black you all agree at least, appeared above the base. I was away meeting with the group that runs things over in Maxwell, and I didn't get back 'til this morning to learn what you have all done. Or some of you. Or one of you ..." she spat her words out.

More than upset, she also had five smart zombie corpses on her hands, which was the real issue today.

"Someone saw the blimp and walked outside to look up. Someone forgot that anyone and everyone can be an enemy of ours, and that someone is sitting at the table, I take it. Someone just had those five, and perhaps some of you just stood there and let the blimp float over the base and take two trucks out of the Motor Pool, I understand," she finished up and looked once again around the table.

That did get some nods.

One of the zombies present named Barb said loudly, "We were all so surprised that we just went out to see what the noise was—the engines of that blimp were loud. The blimp made a small circle, and then it shot at us—and we all ran but some not as fast as others," she said.

That got nods from all at the table.

"So let me see if I understand this. We are the smart zombies here on Ceti4. We are the ones who, yes, were affected by the Boathi virus bombs, but we did not die, and we did not only partially recover like the dumb zombies. In fact, the only difference between us and those who were not affected at all by the Boathi virus is that we eat flesh only. Our brains supposedly were not changed at all. So that means that you all—every single one of you—forgot that we have enemies, and you went out onto the street to be a target. I'd call that dumb ..." she said, and she glared at them all once again.

Barb said, "They're terrible shots—they had like a dozen of us and got only five ..."

Again, heads around the table nodded, and again, Rita slapped the table, and they all jerked once more.

"Thank God for that ... you idiots. I should put you all out in the barracks with our bitten cousins ... as I doubt there's much brain power at the table," she said as she rose and went over to the window in the low, one-story building.

She looked across the base street to the rows of barracks on the other side of the street. There, in the first three of the buildings, their dumb zombie cousins were being held for delivery to other jurisdictions. The army base was used to hold dumb zombies, gathered by their smarter cousins, and then once bitten, they were taught to use language and arms again. Once trained, they were sent with a smarter cousin to new towns and cities. It was a chore, she knew, to try to even train these zombies to be smarter, but it could be done, and all it appeared to take was time. And effort. And more time.

She turned back to the table and stood behind her chair looking at her charges at the table.

"The Motor Pool and its cache of trucks is no longer a secret. We must protect it from all further incursions, and we must be forceful too. I want there to be new security details out at the base entry points, at the Motor Pool doors, up on the roof of the Motor Pool as well. Plus, we do have two guard towers, and I want them manned all three shifts every single day from today and on wards."

Barb partly raised her hand to question her, and Rita nodded to her.

"Would I be correct to think that each of these new security details would be manned by our own bitten zombies—plus at least one of us too?" Barb asked.

She had done the math—will have to watch that one, Rita thought and realized they just didn't have enough smart zombies to watch their bitten cousins. Not nearly enough.

Rita nodded to her. "Yes, you're correct, Barb. We'll all have to pitch in while I get more help from our communities and more personnel. 'Til then, it's up to us. But not a single truck will leave this base. That's a fact. Get to it," she said, and the remaining smart zombies on the base rose and left hurriedly to get the new security details up and running.

Rita had other tasks however. They'd always known the trucks inside the Motor Pool building were there because the government had used them to hoard as much food items as could be trucked to the base in those days during the bombardments just after the Boathi attacks. The food items brought had been much more than whatever storage areas lay behind the huge closed doors inside the building, and it had been left in hundreds of dollies at first.

Someone, maybe via some kind of gossip, had made the Motor Pool a target for local tribes, however, and usually once or twice a year, groups of tribesmen and women stormed the base and made off with the contents of a few dollies.

*No big losses,* Rita thought, *but someone involved in those raids might put two and two together and realize that the rows of doors inside the building held more food.* So far, no attempts had been made to pry open the doors—there were some small marks on one of the doors and a crowbar had been left on the floor ... but no entry had been made.

If they knew those doors were controlled from the console over in the guard shack at the entry point to the base, it might have been different. If zombies could eat what was inside might be different too, but the food items being held there are of no value to us ... but we do have some chips to play with the normals—those Ceti4 citizens who were unaffected by the Boathi virus.

*We protect the Motor Pool.* I'll send out a pickup truck with a couple of bitten cousins and Barb to gather some new smarts, and we'll get by...

##### 

Vera came down the final flight of stairs into the

sub-basement of the big Regime Armories building
and turned to her right to go toward the armory
itself. She'd been summoned and it had been a
summons that meant there was a problem with the
new team.

She strode down the hallway and then turned to
her left to go into the huge room, loaded with all
kinds of weapons. It was one of the real strengths of
the Regime, in that they had inherited the whole
city of Arlington, and it had a large armories
building stocked with just about everything one
might need to govern—by force, that was.

She almost grinned at that, and she was happy
that such a task was hers to help govern.

At the doorway, Gemma and Nixon of the Circle
group that ran the Regime awaited her.

Gemma nodded and spoke first. "We're getting
some real feedback—negative feedback—from
some of the team members, Vera. Thought you
might like to listen in and offer up some arguments
that counteract their POV," she said quietly.

The three of them moved into the room. Inside
near the front of the space was a huge table, where
arms were stacked and backpacks lay half-packed
as they were being worked on. Piles of ammunition,
long guns, handguns, and even ordnance lay there
in separated piles.

In front of the table, the chief armorer stood with

his hands on his hips and a scowl on his face. He obviously was having some issues with the ten men lined up in front of him at the table.

"I do not care what your sense of right and wrong are—these are the items requested by the Circle itself for you to take along on the mission. It does, as you can see, include some small tactical bombs, able to be preset with demolition times to allow you to clear out of the radius of the damage zones. But this is all that you can take. There are no personal choices when it comes to ordnance items," he said, and it sounded like he'd said it already a few times.

The team almost to a man shook their heads negatively.

"Not an answer we are happy with, as we want more firepower," one said.

Vera stepped forward and smiled at the chief armorer and then to the team across the large, wide table.

"Problems, I hear, in the outfitting of the team," she said calmly. She knew that her position as the head of the Circle would get her some respect and that helped. But she also knew that at times, just being a woman was a problem, so she always tried to be polite at first. Before the shit hits the fan, that is, she thought.

She sidled right up to the edge of the table,

hoisted a hip up on one side, and looked at her chief armorer, the man to whom the arming of all Regime teams fell to as his job.

He didn't salute, as that was a long gone military nicety, but he did dip his head before he spoke. "Ma'am, the team has had their own choices for all arms—long guns and hand guns. But the ordnance, as you know, was spec'd in by the Circle. Small, tactical only sized charges, nothing above twenty feet for the concussion zone. No incendiary devices or fragmentation devices were spec'd in—the ones that these team members can carry are for anti-personnel use only. Throw and duck outside of the twenty-foot zone is what they've got. But not what they want, it appears, Ma'am," he said, and his hands were back on his hips again, she noted.

Vera looked over at the team and said, "Team leader, you want to argue this point, please do."

One of the team members, down the table from her, slid along his side of the table to face her directly. He looked over at the chief armorer for a moment and then shrugged. "Ma'am, this mission to go to Walkerville and steal some trucks sounds pretty easy. Intel reports—as you well know—that there may be some zombies tottering all over the old army base. That's not what worries us, Ma'am. What worries us is that it's so easy to kill dumb zombies that the ordnance you offer is irrelevant.

But what, Ma'am, might happen if there are those bitten zombies there, ones who can use arms—or worse, their cousins the smart zombies who have the same brainpower we do. For them, yes, concussion bombs or grenades as they used to be called will work. But we also want the rights to carry frag grenades too—and yes, even incendiary ones too, in case we need to fire a building for instance as a diversion issue so we can get to those trucks. We want all the power we can have, 'Ma'am … and as we're the ones who are out in the field, we would hope you'd see our POV."

He spoke well, Vera thought.

He made good points, and yes, it was a strong argument.

"I think you've made your point, team leader. Therefore, I will instruct the chief armorer to allow you to take any kind of ordnance that you'd wish along with you on your mission.

"But I want you to remember this. A concussion bomb—grenade, yes they're also called that—will kill people. As will a frag grenade too, but at a much bigger kill zone setting. But the incendiary grenades burn—at almost 3,000 degrees, they burn everything that they touch. And you're going to be fighting, I'd imagine, in a closed room with hundreds of trucks full of gasoline. If that's not a recipe for a huge conflagration, then I don't know what is.

"You can take them along as well … but I preach caution. Using one will cause a huge fire … you have been warned—and more than that, you are now all aware that you are the authors of your own future. I'd like to see them all come back unused, but that's, of course, up to you to decide during the mission itself."

She motioned to the chief armorer to allow his aides to go and get the other kinds of bombs for the team to choose from as well, and she turned to leave.

At the doorway, she looked at Gemma and Nixon who'd followed her. "I want the files for all of these team members on my tablet by end of business today. They leave, I think, today, yes?" she asked, and that got her a nod.

She climbed the three flights of stairs back up to the ground floor of the Armories building and paused in the lobby to look out on the street. Bright sunlight, some citizens walking, and she could see a mother pushing a stroller with a child inside who looked positively angelic even at this distance.

She sighed. The Regime was responsible for so much more than keeping Arlington safe … but that was surely at the foundation of our existence …

#####

*Quarters were nice but spartan,* Javor thought as he looked at himself in the mirror on the bathroom wall above the sink. He needed a haircut for sure. His graying temples especially and the matching eyebrows could use some evening up as well. *No real new scars on the face that would last,* he said to himself, as he carefully daubed at the small scratches left by a fir branch that had sideswiped him this morning. *No scars. Good.*

His hands were bad though—chapped flesh, plenty of new scars, and even what looked like a wart on one finger. He grinned at that and said, "You could always tell a lot about a man by his hands." From what he saw as he turned them from palms up to backs up was that he'd been out and about and there was no doubt about that.

He wet his hands and dragged them through his too long hair, hoping that would make it somewhat better. It didn't and he shrugged as he went back out to the main area in the barracks. Here, he and the rest of them had been quartered in what might be called clean but very lean rooms. He had a double that he shared with Sue, Wayne, and Bruce across from the main living area, and the three patrollers were in a bunk bed room just down the hall.

He smiled at Bixby, who was lying on the bed that was his, and he poured out a big helping of kibble for the dog and scratched him behind the ears. The dog would stay here and remain behind for the dinner, and he'd let him out later when he returned. He left his room and closed the door behind him to keep Bixby from troubles.

The rest of the group was in the main living area. Three couches and a kitchen table with six chairs were all that was there, but he knew at least that it was clean and dry and there were no bugs. He scratched behind one ear where a "no-see-um" had gotten him sometime last night, the welt large and scabby already. "Don't scratch," he could remember his mother saying over and over and over. But he still scratched them then, and he scratched now too.

They looked at each other, and Wayne, of course, made the first comment.

"As an ambassador for the Regime, I think we're like way under dressed, unclean, and to be totally honest, I think we're out of our depth." He looked at Sue when he said that, and that got him a smile.

"Well put, Wayne. Mostly true too—but after the Boathi made Ceti4 into Bones, I'm afraid being under dressed is how we all feel. Unclean, well, there appears to be no showers in the head, and as far as being out of our depth—that's not true at all. We are the ones who were charged by the Circle to ask the Empire to forgo its slavery model. That's all we're to do here. Ask them, argue with them, and get them to see the light. And if not, then oh well … we go to Plan B," she said.

They all nodded. Plan B, as had been explained to them at the meeting with the Circle, was to eliminate the leadership of the Empire. In any way, shape, or form, but that should put the cult into chaos and that too might work. Perhaps, it was the leader and his intimate group of aides who wanted the slave model to be how they ran the Empire. It was really Plan Z as far as Javor was concerned, as the simple fact was that while it might be easy to take out the leaders of the Empire, it was a suicide mission for the team.

"I'm carrying my Colt," Javor admitted, "but hidden behind my back."

The rest of the group nodded. All were still armed but had their weapons concealed. As they were all pondering that, a knock on the door to their barracks building sounded, and a black-robed disciple came in.

"You are required to have dinner now with the prime disciple at your audience. Please follow me," he said and turned to leave the room.

"Can we leave our items here?" Sue asked. "They'll be okay, right?" she said with a teensy bit of anxiety in her voice.

"They will not be touched at all," he said over his

shoulder as he went out the front door and down the short walkway to the street outside.

They all followed him, and while it went unsaid, the four Shieldsmen, armed with shotguns, who trailed along behind weren't mentioned at all. *Seems like they trust us, but maybe not so much,* Javor thought and grinned.

They walked down the short street to the main street of Empire City, turned to the right, and then walked toward the pyramid. From here, the structure, though it was still being built, was impressive as hell. The shine of sunlight, even now coming up to dusk, was bright off the granite, and they could see teams of slaves still hauling the large stones up the ramp on the rows of rolling logs. He tried to see the slaves themselves to see how they looked, but they were just too far away to take any kind of an audit of their condition. A quick count showed that he could see more than what he guessed were four hundred slaves, all straining on ropes as big as his forearm was thick.

"About how many slaves does the Empire have building the pyramid?" he asked very casually.

The answer was not surprising, actually.

"That is a question you might want to ask the prime disciple," the black-robed man ahead of him threw back over his shoulder.

*Figures,* Javor thought, *that they might want that to*

*be kept to themselves. No sense letting that information get out there,* he reasoned. *Intel of any kind was a good thing for the other side—in this case, the Regime—to have.*

They walked slowly but soon were in front of a building almost at the last corner before where the pyramid was being erected. Their leader led them inside the main doorway, up a large flight of stairs, and into what might have been a meeting room. Inside the room, there were Shieldsmen stationed around the room at the walls, and Javor counted a dozen of them.

But tonight it was set with a large round table and place settings for dinner. A quick count showed there were only eight place settings.

*Us and one more,* Javor thought, and as their leader told them to sit, they all did that.

Sue got Jon to change seats with her so that she was sitting directly opposite the only seat not taken at the table, and Javor nodded at that strategy.

Well done, Sue, he thought as he reached for his water and swallowed the very cold icy water with pleasure.

They sat. They fidgeted for more than ten minutes, and the only thing that happened was that a steward kept refilling the pitchers of ice water that were on the tables whenever they had a drink of same. There was nothing to do but to wait.

148

From a doorway behind a large tapestry of a forest scene on the wall, a black-robed man appeared, and he slowly walked to the empty place at the table and smiled at them all before he seated himself.

"Welcome to the Forest Empire," he said nicely as he sat and got comfortable, "and yes, I am the prime disciple—the head of the Empire." He looked in turn at each of them, face to face.

"Let us eat first, and get to know each other— would help perhaps in what comes after, no?" he said, again nicely, and that got nods and yeses from around the table.

And what a dinner it was, they all felt. Tonight wasn't cold or chemically heated MREs. The starter course was smoked fish draped over a terrine of vegetables with Cumberland sauce sprinkled over top. The main courses were either a fillet of what looked like beef or a kind of fish he'd never heard of, so he took the fish. Salads, a chunk of great sourdough bread, and even a desert that he had to pass on came along in their time.

And the prime disciple talked to them. He spent some time on their history of how they had found that their God had sent his minions, the Boathi, Javor called them, to bomb and burn their world. He explained how their God made most of the non-believers die, and of the ones that lived, most turned into zombies of all types. He shared that the Forest Empire had risen slowly, but being here in the north, isolated from most of the major cities and populations below the boreal forests, meant they were spared from most of the deaths that infected the rest of the planet.

The prime disciple told them that because the areas in which the Empire ruled were also areas where huge deposits of oil and gas had been discovered and been mined and stored already, the Empire had its own sources of power built in. Added to that, their ownership of the oil and gas dirigibles meant they had air power too.

He was open with all of that, Javor thought. He seemed to never correct his points as he spoke or try to backpedal either, but in fact, he shared all.

Sue asked some pointed questions too, and they got answers as well.

The Empire had more than five thousand slaves right now and more on the way. The pyramid was the major reason they were after new slaves. The trucks had come from Walkerville, the prime disciple had responded when Sue had asked where they came from.

*Quite open and honest,* Javor thought.

The prime disciple put down his small spoon as he'd finished his dessert, which was similar to bananas Foster. He smiled as the stewards cleared the table. He pushed his chair back a bit and waved for more water, and two stewards rushed to get him a new pitcher.

The prime disciple looked over at Sue and said, "So, I understand you represent the Regime. May I ask what brings you to Empire City to see me?"

Sue nodded, then leaned forward, and smiled at the Prime Disciple. "Prime, we—the Regime that is —find that the planet is slowly re-building itself. Our potential is great, our future is bright," she started with, and that was all true.

"But what worries the Regime, Prime, is the fact that the Empire has slaves. Buys slaves, uses slaves, well, like slaves to build your pyramid this week and God knows what next week," she said.

The prime disciple nodded and commented, "Yes, God does know what we'd need next week too," but that didn't slow Sue down.

"The Regime believes that slavery is so wrong, so not us—that we are here today making a formal request for the Forest Empire to cease and desist using slaves. That all current slaves be released— given food and clothing to allow them to return to their homes or wherever they might like to go. And that the Empire, from now on, never uses slaves again. We, as ambassadors from the Regime, ask the Empire to consider this request," she finished her formal statement, and she leaned back into her chair.

That part of her job was done. And now for the answer.

The prime disciple stared at her, and his face was neither smiling nor frowning. He just looked at her as he reached for his glass of water.

He took a big sip and then put the glass down and motioned for a colder pitcher, Javor thought, only for an instant, as each of the Shieldsmen around them at the table brought their spears up and were ready to charge the table...

# CHAPTER SEVEN

Sue spoke first.

"I see that your, what, Shieldsmen, I believe they are called, have changed their stances. They now appear to be threatening—do I have that right Mr. Prime Disciple?" she said.

Not a soul at the table had moved, though all the cadre was armed.

Javor thought, *I'd have just about enough time to reach around to my back, draw out the Colt, and plug the spearman in front of me—but not behind me, for sure.*

*He knew that with more spears in the room than their group, he was in jeopardy. They all were.*

This is a standoff, he thought, and he was glad the rest of his group had had the same reasoning about the crisis they were in.

The prime disciple smiled at them all. He spoke

slowly and yet firmly. "We, the Forest Empire, know that the Regime is full of non-believers. They are a nation of non-believers, so what they want is immaterial to us. But what we want is what we will do—we will be the future rulers of Ceti4, and we will do it with slaves. You all in fact should know that we will do just that—and you will help. You are now slaves of the Forest Empire—Shieldsmen, take them away," he said.

He didn't move, but the Shieldsmen did, each taking only a few steps to put their spear tips right up against the backs of the cadre team members' necks. Javor froze as they all did. *Spears at such close quarters would be deadly. These were trained spearmen, and he had no recourse but to sit still.* From a side doorway that now opened, more of these Shieldsmen appeared, and they searched each one of the cadre team members' bodies. Guns were gathered, and a probe was taken from one of the patrollers. As they had each of them stand, they patted them all down, and Wayne lost his ankle gun as well.

Sue tried to speak, but the prime disciple held up a hand to stop her. "You are now property of the Forest Empire. I think I'll have you sent to the pyramid ramps, where you'll all be under constant surveillance, and have you learn what it takes to move stones into position, and you will all help to create our pyramid, our crowning glory," he said and pushed back from the table.

Sue yelled at him. "Prime Disciple—we are ambassadors from the Regime. You cannot, with any degree of impunity, do anything to us—we must be allowed to return to Arlington. This is an illegal act, Prime—it is an act of war," she claimed loudly over and over.

The prime disciple nodded to her. "We do agree on that—we are at war with the Regime; I'm so surprised that you didn't already know that. Slaves. You'll all make wonderful slaves, strong pullers, and if you do well, you might even get an extra helping of your dinners. Too bad that such fare will not equal the wonderful repast we just had.

He walked a few feet away and then turned back to them. "The dog, Khuno, has been re-assigned to our canine teams; your bags will be searched, and then some of the clothing will be put into your new slave barracks. You are slaves as of now. Get used to it," he said, and he laughed loudly.

"Khuno was never yours—he was a Shorecroft Patrol K9 dog," Jon said.

"And what makes you think that means anything —we provide dogs to many other towns and villages for their use. Khuno was sent to Shorecroft just a year ago, it seems, and it's nice to see that he's back. He'll go out again too, and be our own secret within another new town and their security forces. We seed many dogs, Khuno was just one of them," he said as he shook his head.

"You all must think that we believers are just a cult, full of idiots who pray all day long. Some of us are, but here at the top, not so much, eh?" he questioned.

Everyone in the room knew that question needed no answers. They had thought just that, and they'd just been outdone by this cult, and outdone badly.

As the Shieldsmen led them out of the building, instead of turning back to their left toward the city, they went to their right toward the pyramid. At the start of the construction site, they turned right once again.

Along that street, in the almost dark early evening, they were marched, and occasionally they went by Empire City citizens who all stood out of their way. Behind their hands, they talked to each other about them, Javor thought. With at least twenty shieldsmen holding them at spear point, it was no wonder.

At the next corner on this long block, they turned to their left and entered an area that had a tall wire fence all around it. A set of guards let them into the area, and ahead there were low single-story buildings—slave barracks. They were marched and prodded all the way down to the last one on the left and then herded inside.

A large room, bathrooms against the far end wall, with two dozen bunk beds was what they found. At a set of tables all pushed together, four other slaves were wolfing down their dinner. They turned to look at the cadre's entrance but didn't stop eating, gobbling up what looked like some kind of stew.

The Shieldsmen stopped, and one stepped forward. "You are slaves. We have chosen to bed you with other discontents and non-believers here in this barracks," he said as he pointed at the four slaves still eating.

"You will obey, or you will be whipped. If you are whipped too often or if you injure yourself— you will go on the list for the next Equinox Games. You have few chances—I'd offer that you do not want to spend them unwisely." He and the rest of the Shieldsmen turned to leave.

"What makes you think that we will do this?" Sue said, stepping up to challenge him.

The spear caught her in the shoulder, its tip and inches more of steel embedded just below her collar bone, blood seeping out.

"We do not think at all, we know," the Shieldsman said as one of them moved forward to pull the spear out, and he wiped it off on her hip as the rest of them held the cadre at spear point.

"You will be visited by the slave keeper in a

157

while, but 'til then, I'd try to staunch that blood loss. You will need to pull tomorrow and pull mightily too. Does anyone else wish to question the Empire?" he said.

The quiet was pregnant with hate, but not a word came out of the members of the cadre.

He nodded. "This barracks will always have its own guards, but the whole slave camp is guarded. Shieldsmen and dogs and yes, slaves earn extra food if they turn in those planning to escape. Your time here is yours, but the other half a day is spent helping the Empire build the pyramid ..." he said, and in a moment, they'd left the barracks building.

Wayne and Bruce were already at Sue's side, helping her to lie down. Wayne ripped off his shirt, tearing an arm off and using it as a temporary bandage to soak up her blood. She was actually better than they all thought—no screaming or any type of reaction. Shock, Javor thought at first.

"Point had pretty sharp edges, but no barbs," Wayne said as he plied the wound itself.

Sue looked up and him, grinned, and said, "What, Wayne, no one, two, three count?"

He shook his head and then looked up and over to the table where the other slaves were still eating but all had eyes on Sue.

"Can any of you help here?" Wayne said.

They stopped chewing, and one of them, a big

158

man with a dusty T-shirt on, put down his spoon. "Slave keeper will be here sometime soon—spear wounds go to the top of the list," he said.

Jon said, "I take it that the slave keeper will provide some kind of medical help?"

"Some kind, yes," the big man said as he got up slowly as if he was hurting himself.

He limped over, and Javor could see he favored his left leg and was moving slowly. He got to Sue's side and bent over to look at the wound itself.

"Typical, they aim below the clavicle to ensure that tomorrow you can still shoulder the rope and pull," he said, and then he pointed at the edges of the wound.

"See that yellow tinge? Ointment that they put on their spear tips, helps the wound by killing any germs—sorta like they want to hurt you, but you gotta pull tomorrow," he said with what might have been an attempt at irony.

Javor nodded. *Made sense.* He took a step toward the man and held out his hand.

"Javor Novak—thanks for your help," he said as he introduced the whole cadre to the man.

The big guy nodded to them all and even smiled a little. "I'm Toby Nelson—been here over a year. Last member of the original oil exploration team who got jumped northwest of here near New Liskeard. I was one of the floater pilots for the company, and now the Empire has them all. All my peers are gone, but I'm still here. If you're smart, then you'll just pull, eat, and then sleep.

"Wound's gonna hurt like hell for a week or so—but will heal okay, I think. Slave keeper will stitch it up and put in some more antiseptic. Pulling tomorrow, Sue, will be hell, I can show you how to fake it. One day, we'll all give you, but the slack will get us all whipped some …"

He again shrugged and went back to the table to finish his stew. "Hungry?" he asked as he eyed the big bowl of remaining stew and the new slaves to the barracks.

Jon said, "No, we've just eaten."

Toby grinned and took another portion onto his plate. "More for us," he said with another grin, and the whole table refilled their plates.

Sue moaned more in the next hour as they slowly acclimatized to their new living quarters.

"I like the other place better," Bruce said, and that got more nods than anything else said that night.

They all helped get Sue over to a lower bunk and arranged her on it. She winced badly but didn't cry out, and she waited for medical attention.

"Something I have to tell you all," she said, first making sure the slaves were all at the table still eating and that she had a bit of privacy.

"The Regime gave me something to help us negotiate," she said with a wink.

Javor thought she might have been somewhat wonky from the wound, so he patted her other shoulder and said, "Easy, Sue ... easy."

She shook him off and in a low whisper—so low they all had to bend down and get close to her as she exhaled her words softly—she said, "The Regime gave me a nuke—it should be in my pack, disguised as a simple battery for the radio. Half-mile spread, no rads either, so it's really just to do a single task of blowing up this city. If I don't make it, you should know it exists." Her body spasmed then with pain.

Bruce held her one arm on the wound side and said, "Nothing doing, Sue ... you're going to be fine. You heard that guy, they don't hurt slaves who can pull ... just settle down, honey."

Wayne and Javor nodded and patted her too.

Ten minutes later, a group of Shieldsmen entered carrying their packs and tossed them in a heap just inside the doorway. Bruce went over, checked, came back in a moment, and said, "Most of my stuff is still there, but it has been rifled through."

Sue asked about her pack, and he nodded and said, "Yup, all your stuff is there—but the radio looks like it has seen better days, but all else is about the same. Your undies look like they've been handled too ..."

That got a grunt from some of them and a smile to,o which was what Bruce had been aiming at, and they waited now for medical help.

Javor grabbed a lower bunk right beside Sue and realized there was only a thin mattress over the metal slats that were the bed frame itself. He found his clothing on the floor, gathered it up, and put it on his bed,to use as a pillow. His backpack had been slit open by the Shieldsmen, he thought, and rifled through. No kibble for Bixby—and that at least was only a small disappointment, as he knew the dog would be well treated. He did wonder how a dog could be used against the master that he'd adopted, and that bugged him for a while as he watched the rest of the cadre settle in.

Twenty minutes later, a black-robed figure along with three Shieldsmen walked into the barracks, and he went right over to Sue. Kneeling beside her, he pressed and prodded the wound, ignoring her squeals of pain. His face never showed a thing as he went into a satchel he had over his shoulder and got out a tube of something. He leaned over Sue, and pressing the area around the hole with one hand, he squeezed some of the ointment out of the tube and right into the hole. He went back into his bag and withdrew a small leather case from which he took a needle and some kind of catgut or the like, Javor thought.

He was all business as he used a spray to topically numb the area around the wound, and then he stitched up the wound with stitch after stitch. Javor counted eleven stitches to close Sue's wound.. The black-robed man then went back into his bag and used some thick bandages and some wide white tape to seal the wound. He fished out a couple of pills, gave them to Wayne, who was hovering over them both, and nodded.

"One now, one tomorrow at first pull, and then the last one at dinner," the man said.

Sue was full of questions, but he ignored her. Wayne just nodded and the slave keeper left them as he'd come, quietly and quickly.

Sue moaned and Wayne stuffed the first pill into her, and she had to work up the spit to swallow it.

"We have water—we always have lots of water," Toby said as he got up and walked over with a cup in his hand, and Sue took it gratefully and drank the whole cupful.

Bruce took the bunk over Sue, and Wayne took the one over Javor. They all sat and chatted. The patrollers took the next couple of bunks, and they discussed their plight as well as what they might do about it.

"Thing is, is that the barracks are all wired so that the Empire can hear you all the time. Good thing too, because if we heard you all discussing a plan of escape, we'd need to report it—or be whipped. Glad to hear that you're all sad you're here, but that's about as far as it should go, I'd think," Toby voiced from his own bunk at the far end.

*All good to know,* Javor said to himself. *Very good indeed ... Now what I need is sleep, as tomorrow I get to help build a pyramid ... sadly ...*

#####

*Jon was right ahead of him,* and Javor thought, *in the past week or so that we've been slaves, his back muscles have already grown considerably.*

While the guards were smart enough to make the team work on alternating sides of the ropes, that was due, he thought, to just trying to balance out the slaves' muscle tone and abilities. It was the smart thing to do, and that worried him a bit. Anyone who showed that kind of planning for their slaves meant they had been at this for a while—and would continue too.

*One week and a bit,* he thought, *is really not enough time to try to formulate an escape plan.*

That's what he told himself as his head hit his bunk every night, tired to the bone.

*We have no weapons. We are watched every minute we're awake—and when we sleep as well. We have no one here who we can use to try to gain an advantage to help escape either. We are what we are, slaves ...*

He was a puller. Everyone who was a slave, he'd learned, had a job title, which was descriptive of what their job was.

There were pullers—like him. His team was his barracks mates—the cadre plus Toby and the others —and they always pulled on one huge rope on their side of the sledge for a full day. Another team just like them, but one bigger at twelve slaves, took the other side of the sledge on their own rope, and everyone pulled.

Moving the rollers from the back of the sledge around to the front of the sledge were the rollers. He almost grinned at that name being a bit more descriptive than the job entailed as the rollers waited behind the sledge for a large log to come free. It was picked up by four rollers, moved to one side, and then run up past the sledge for it to be positioned in front of the sledge as the next rolling log to provide almost frictionless upward movement on the ramp.

There were mudders too, whose job it was to daub the rollers with a coating of mud—not the whole log but just above the three rails on which the logs rolled. Friction was the enemy, and Javor had to admit, the Empire had covered just about all their bases.

He knew that behind him and below him and

miles away, there was the granite quarry, with more slaves who cut the blocks from the granite walls. Those slaves moved the blocks the three miles from quarry to the pyramid itself. And then finally, the pullers, like him, who slowly moved stone by stone upward toward the summit.

He grunted as one foot on the ramp below slipped just a bit and the rope took some slack. He flinched ahead of time knowing this kind of slack meant a guard could well be drawing back on his whip right now ... and in a moment more, he'd feel the tip sting into his back.

But not this time. No whip cracked and he pulled a bit harder on the rope—not hard enough to cause any slack to appear in front of him either. He'd learned that the rope told the guards who was pulling steadily and who was not. And their whips corrected all.

He pulled on the rope steadily with about eighty percent of what he figured was his maximum pulling ability. This stone, the fourth since they'd started this morning, was the same size as always. With twenty-three pullers on the mud-covered logs, the sledge made solid time up and up and up. At the corners, the ramp leveled so that the pryers could pry-bar it around the corner, and they got to stand and take a few minutes while the sledge was turned the ninety degrees.

He nodded to Wendy, one of the new barracks mates he'd inherited, and smiled over to Toby. They were a couple, he thought, having heard tiptoe footsteps in the night, but that was none of his business. He had to pull. That was all.

And that's what bothered him the most.

*Being a slave of the Empire is not something I'd ever thought I would do — I know what I could do. But the plan to escape is still beyond me.*

"They said that there'd be more facing stones again soon," Wayne said under his breath to him so that the guards didn't overhear them. Slaves do not talk — they pull; he'd been whipped more than a dozen times learning that one.

He nodded. Facing stones were lighter as they came to the ramp with one side already beveled off. They'd become the exterior stones of the pyramid, and yes, they were easier to pull. He could turn to look way down to see if he could find any such stones in the assembly points to come up the ramp, but he didn't bother. Today, they had to get ten stones up the ramp and in place for the final pryers to get into position and the fitters to make the proper installation too.

He sweated more and held up his hand to show the water girls that he needed more water, and one of them, a youngster of about ten or so years, came over with the big plastic bag now half-full of water.

She motioned, he squatted down, and she aimed the spout on the side at his mouth. Lukewarm water surged out of the bag and into his mouth. A week ago, he'd forgotten to care that this was messy and made him look like a boor—water was what he needed, so he drank and then held up a hand to get her to stop.

He smiled at her as he stood back up and said, "Thank you," and a guard near him barked, "Shut up, slave," and he did just that.

He saw that the pryers had the sledge now in great position, running on the rails below, and he got ready in line for the big pull that was always needed to start a new pull up a new side of the pyramid. They always had to start off with a huge pull to get the sledge up and on the first rolling log —pryers pryed and they pulled and the rollers stuffed in that first log—and they were off at a foot or a bit less every few seconds, climbing the pyramid with another stone.

No escape. The future for him was as a slave …

"Nonsense," he said to himself again today, "I will find a way out of this." Every member of the cadre felt, he was sure, like he did right now. They pulled. But behind that pull was the raw emotion that they would try to escape.

Every day, Sue said she wondered what he Regime was doing about their disappearance, and

the answer today was just like it had been then—
they had no idea.

*Wonder how Bixby is doing once again here in the
city, or maybe he's already been sent out again Wonder
if one of those facing stones might be next,* Javor
thought and hoped the load could be lighter for a
while...

##### 

He held up his hand, and the water girl he liked
to see, the ten-year old girl with the blonde hair,
hauled the water bag over past a couple of guards
who were sitting on a roller log and toward him.

The pryers were doing their thing—jamming
their long pry bars under the edge of the sledge
itself and gently lifting it up on the rails below.
They did so carefully to not damage the underside
of the sledge, which might affect its ability to roll
smoothly on the rolling logs. They were careful to
move the sledge inch by inch, so the alignment
would be met and not exceeded.

The guard with the black hair, streaked now with
rock dust, stopped the girl and asked where, and
she pointed at first Sue, over on the far side of the
pile of log rollers, and then to him. The guard
nodded, eyed him, and pursed his lips together.

Javor had tasted that guard's whip quite a few

times already this week, and for the past three weeks that he'd been a puller, he thought that given all the hate that was building up inside him, he'd love to square off against the man.

*About my size but twenty years younger*, he thought. *Should be enough of a chance for him to live past round one.* He grinned and turned away.

In front of him, the rails that the sledge ran on were lying on the solid ramp, flecked and spotted with mud. Beyond them lay only about ten feet of ramp, and then it fell away the seventy or eighty feet down the side of the already built part of the pyramid below him. Over there, some of the other team of pullers were milling about, waiting for the pryers off to his left to do their job.

It was only going to take a minute or so more for them to have the sledge properly positioned for the big pull, and Javor turned to see that Sue was still getting a drink from the water girl. She was thirsty, he thought, and though he'd love to have a couple of mouthfuls of water, it looked like it wouldn't be at this stop. But Sue finished quickly and urged the water girl to go over to him.

"No time for more water," the black-haired guard said. "Get ready for the big log pull-up."

While the pryers were still prying, the water girl seemed to know that he was too early for that, and she skirted around him and danced over to Javor

170

quickly. He'd backed up to stand now right behind the sledge between the rails themselves, and he grinned at her as he did that deep knee bend to squat and receive some water just before the next pull. He closed his eyes and tilted his head backward.

The crack of the whip was loud, and as the black-haired guard laid a big crack on the water girl's back, she cried out and staggered to her left.

Javor hadn't seen it happen, but he knew the sound of a whip lash, and the water girl brushed by him on his right as she fled the whip.

It cracked again and caught her squarely on her back, Javor saw. As she bent over to try to flee, the water bag dropped off her shoulder and leaked all over the ramp. She got a couple of more strides in before Javor dove backward towards her, and he caught her just before she went over the side of the ramp to fall down the side of the smooth pyramid.

He scrabbled at her arm. The one he held was wet with spilled water and so small. He was just making good on his grip when the whip cracked again, and he felt it hit him in the face, just above his left eye.

He almost let go of the girl, but he managed to hold on as two more cracks of the same whip caught him once on the chest and once on the arm holding the water girl who hung over the edge of the ramp now.

He gripped the edge of the muddy rail with his right thigh and calf, and he tried to pull her back up and over the edge of the ramp. The black-haired guard strode by him to whip the girl up close now. Javor's alien knee was straining, but he knew he could count on it to keep him anchored.

He grabbed a handful of the small stone gravel that the ramp was made from, and with an overhand toss, he threw it at the guard who stopped in mid-wind-up of his whip to see where that cloud of gravel had come from—and he turned now to whip Javor.

Javor squeezed with all his might on his right knee, and that pulled him and the girl back off the edge of the ramp. He took another whip blow to his shoulder, but the blood on his face made it difficult to see the guard as it flowed into his eyes. He stood and jumped on his right leg so quickly that all the guard saw was an attacking slave, and the guard stepped back.

And he back-stepped off the edge of the ramp and fell down the side of the pyramid, bouncing every so often on the smooth sides, but the sound of him stopping on the flat stone mezzanine at the pyramid's base was loud. He didn't move, Javor noted, as he heard more commotion behind him, and he turned.

Three guards and two Shieldsmen had his cadre
of friends held at spear point. They'd been trying to
intervene, he figured, and only the bare points of
steel had held them back. Wayne and Bruce were
lying face down with Shieldsmen holding them
down using their spears.

"This is—was—an accident … I saw it, we all
saw it—let's get back to the big pull," Sue said as
she tried to deflect whatever was coming.

And Javor just stood there, quiet now, with a
hand across the water girl's shoulders as she sobbed
beside him.

In less than a minute, a whole squad of
Shieldsmen appeared running up the ramp, and
three moved him back to the edge of the ramp so
that one could approach him and put on shackles.
He nodded and said, "I will not resist—this really
was just an accident."

Moments later, he was being marched down the
ramp past other pullers and teams still moving
blocks of stone up the pyramid.. The march toward
the base of the pyramid took him past other guards
who all catcalled at him and called for his head.
They passed by other slaves who looked away from
him to avoid any eye contact which might have
brought a whipping. Whenever Javor was marched
past other Shieldsmen, they stared at him, shock
and horror filling their eyes.

173

At the bottom of the pyramid, they marched him in quick time back to the slave barracks camp, and he thought for a moment that he'd simply be put in his barracks, but they walked him right by. They moved ahead to a solidly fenced location past the slave barracks and turned in to their left.

He could hear dogs barking. He could hear shouts and even once in a while he could hear dogs being praised, if he could follow by ear what he couldn't see. This was perhaps where the Empire dogs were kept, and he wondered if he'd see Bixby here.

He was marched down a long pathway of grass, between what looked like dog kennels, and then they stopped while one of them went into a trailer off to the side.

Moments later, he was back, and they continued down the rows of kennels until they reached some that were black. The frost wire fencing on the four walls and the ceiling had been painted black and would keep anything inside, inside.

One opened the cage door, and they thrust him inside. He held out his hands to have them remove the shackles, and that got only a grunt from the one at the cage door as he closed it, locked it, and took the key with him.

Javor watched as they all walked away. He looked at his surroundings. The cage of solid frost wire fencing was about ten feet long by five feet wide. A bowl was in the far corner, and he had no idea if that was for water or for his own waste.

He went down to the far side and slid slowly down the fencing until his ass hit the concrete floor. Just behind him was a small three-foot section of dirt too, but the concrete was warm on his legs, and after the strain earlier, the warmth was what he needed.

He massaged his right knee a bit and was glad it had been able to hold both him and the water girl from the edge of the ramp.

He wondered, of course, *what might come next, but he also knew that whatever it was going to be, it would not be to his liking…*

##### #####

They came through the fence at the rear of the army base, and all ten took a moment to let their night vision goggles get acclimatized to the few lights ahead on the base's main road. It had taken almost an hour to cut a huge hole in the fence emptying a complete span between two of the fence posts. Now they had an unfenced expanse that was twenty feet wide.

Behind the base was a large park or field with some piles of what looked like huge old sewer pipes now abandoned. At the far side of the park, another road led east to the major part of town. This was their escape route. They'd all studied the map and knew exactly where to enter the base, and of course, how to get to the enormous Motor Pool building that lay straight ahead about a half a mile in.

The team leader nodded to his number two and said, "Point … all weapons on full silence, and slow but steady … we have all of nineteen more minutes."

They fanned out into a tactical formation, and they walked gently with as little noise as possible down the road ahead.

Up on the right were the rows of barracks, and they knew that the zombies—smart, dumb, or whatever—slept there. They also knew, after the full day of spying on the base, that there were usually four zombies up ahead guarding the Motor Pool. Two at the doorways and two more up on the roof.

Last night, they had seen that the two on the roof had sat for most of the nighttime hours, nodding off even. But the two on the road just sat on the stack of pallets they'd arranged to block the doorways a bit.

The team trotted ahead and passed the barracks quietly, awakening no one. As the team approached the two guards again still sitting on those pallets, it took them a moment to realize they were being attacked—bitten zombies, the leader noted.

176

He snapped his fingers and from the team members beside him, the two guards dropped as they were still trying to get up, killed by the silenced rifle fire. One of them had almost gotten his gun up to aim at them, and it clattered to the pavement as he dropped back on the pallets underneath him.

Up on the roof a voice called out. "Raphael, what the heck you doing?"

The team leader held up a hand to freeze his team. They waited.

Moments later, a head popped over the side of the roof up about three stories, and a silent bullet took him out.

That left one, they all knew.

The team split up with five of them going into the Motor Pool building to start up five trucks.

From above, the zombie opened fire, and one of the remaining team members down on the road cried out. He was not hit, but he yelped like he had been. Beside him, a team member shot the zombie who'd looked over the edge just a bit, and the body fell off the roof.

"We're live," the team leader yelled, as behind them down the road, they could hear screen doors opening and then slamming closed.

The remaining five of them piled into the building and ran the rows looking for trucks with open doors. The earlier five team members had simply found keys and tried the trucks. If they started, they left them running with the door open.

"We've got nine so far," a voice called out from the rows ahead, and in a moment, it was added to by a new voice that yelled out, "Ten … we've got ten."

The team leader moved to a close truck with the door wide open and got up and into the driver's seat. He revved the engine and then led the way out of the row he was in, turning sharply to the left and then bearing down on the doorway.

In the doorway, however, were zombies—many zombies—but it didn't matter. He floored the truck. It was an army personnel carrier truck, about twenty-five feet long with a huge tarp over the back end that would usually hold troops. "Today, it is a doorway clearing truck," he said to himself as he plowed right into the zombies dead ahead. He noted for later reports that they were of the bitten type—they all had some kind of weapon but not a lot of rifles. One was standing on the far sidewalk as more were running down the road toward the building, and he was aiming at the team leader's truck.

The team leader didn't turn but went right across the road and mowed him down as two bullets hit his truck. He tossed out a frag grenade that went off with a big bang, and zombies toppled behind him.

"One down. A ton to go," he said to himself, and he swung to the right toward the barracks and lined up more zombies. He floored the truck and mowed down as many as he could. Behind him, another truck and then a third truck came out of the Motor Pool building and turned to the right to follow his truck.

Ahead, on one of the walkways to the fifth barracks building, he could see a pair of zombies lying on the grass pointing at his lead truck with rifles. He climbed back up off the road, went around a couple of sapling trees in the way, and aimed the truck at them.

He tossed another frag grenade out the passenger side window, and it went off well behind his truck, but he could hear cries behind too. "Good but now those two ..."

One bullet came through the windshield, and it made a clean hole as it passed right through the cab and then the large tarped area behind him. He leaned on the horn, and the noise made many of the other zombie heads turn. In his rear-view side mirror, he could see more and more trucks coming out of the Motor Pool building. As he looked back ahead, those two zombies were now getting up quickly.

*Quicker,* he thought, *than even bitten zombies could*

*—these are smart zombies and that is news.*

He aimed at the one who split off to the left closer to the barracks building and rode him down, the body banging first on the bumper, and then he made sure to run at least one tire over his enemy.

Behind him now as he was coming up on the hole in the fences they'd cut earlier, the ten trucks were all hauling toward their escape hatch.

He mounted the curb once more and plowed right over a small sapling in his way and out the cut in the fence. Then he angled over to his right toward the first pile of big concrete sewer pipes.

He was out of danger was his first thought, when from the pile of pipes came a fusillade of bullets. Some just hit the truck, but some also hit the cab. He took two shells, one in the right arm and another in the left shoulder.

Makes steering hard, he thought, as he leaned on the horn to play a warning—one short, one long, one short, one long—and he drove on. He tossed out an incendiary grenade to hit the pipes, and in moments, a gigantic wall of flame reached up to the sky.

Behind him, the rest of the trucks went by the same first pile of sewer pipes, now on fire. Two of the trucks slowed and came to rest as their drivers were hit and killed. One more somehow exploded, the engine flaming up with a huge swath of fire.

One truck hit the sewer pipes full tilt, the body of its driver slumped over the steering wheel. That knocked over one end of the now burning pipes and a few dropped down to roll on the ground, effectively stopping the hail of gunfire.

The remaining trucks all made the far end of the field and then turned to the right to take the road to the downtown area. At a corner ahead, the team leader stopped in the lead and got out of his truck to take stock of what had happened. He walked and talked to the remaining six drivers, and then at the end of the line, he looked back over the field in the distance.

A huge pile of flaming sewer pipes and a burning truck was all he could make out, and using his night vision goggles was out as the flames made them unusable.

He nodded. Smart zombies controlled the base. Yes, they'd sent bitten zombies to attack them at the Motor Pool, but they'd also known that there had to be another way out of the base. The main gates were closed and locked, and three trucks barricaded the only road in.

He knew it had to be smart zombies because dumb zombies would never have searched for their exit and sent snipers to lay in wait for them. The zombie snipers had gone through the fence hole the team had created and had used the sewer pipes for ambush cover while they waited for the trucks.

"Smart," he said to himself as one of the team squeezed his shoulder wound to pour in an antiseptic cream and slap a field dressing on it just like he'd just done for his right arm.

"Gotta go," he said to them all, and they started up the trucks and aimed at the town center to turn south to get up on the interstate and head back to Arlington, though there would be some side trips on regional roads too.

*Six ... not as good as ten ... team members ... not the trucks ...*

# CHAPTER EIGHT

He had lain on the dirt corner of his kennel now for three full days. Once a day someone brought water and poured some into the bowl that lay on the concrete floor beside him. Since the sun was so bright and hot, the concrete heated up too much, and the dirt was the coolest spot to sit for hours. *At least*, he said to himself, *the dirt is cooler.*

They never brought him food. "No kibble even," he said to himself, as if such an item could even be called human food, but he knew he'd have wolfed it down none the less.

He sat in the sharp sunlight of full summer all day long—there was no shade anywhere in the kennel areas. He watched other dogs walking their pens, back and forth, over and over, and he wondered about humans and their need to cage animals. He got up every hour or so to stretch and flex his right knee, and it quickly healed from the stress of saving the water girl. The alien tissue that had replaced his some twenty-plus years ago had helped him before and helped him again.

He grinned. He wished that he could have had both knees and even arm joint replacements when he'd been a decathlon champion back then. *Instead of doing a long jump of only forty feet like I could on my own human muscles, wonder what kind of distance I might have been able to get then?*

*Fifty?*

*Sixty maybe?*

He shook his head. *Days gone by,* he thought, and he turned at the very front of his kennel fence to walk the five strides back. He did his ten laps and then sat again for another hour and waited.

After the third day, he had had it with trying to stay anything else but frustrated and upset. He wondered about the guard and if he was dead. He wondered about the little water girl and what they'd done about her. He wondered about his team and what they might be going through as punishment.

He wondered, then closed his eyes for his morning nap time, and slowly faded out …

Bang!

A huge noise that shook the whole frost wired cage on all four sides awoke him, and he leaned forward, shaking his head to see what it was. At the end of the kennel cage stood four Shieldsmen and a robed disciple. He motioned for Javor to come over and so he did.

"We need to take you to see the prime disciple," he said, and he opened the kennel cage door slowly.

"But know this—you will die by spear if you try to do anything other than come along calmly," he said, and while his voice was calm, Javor could hear the steel inside same.

He half-smiled and followed the lead Shieldsman back along the walkway to the street, ignoring the barking dogs and the few dog handlers who moved out of their way.

*Maybe Bixby is here.* He looked at every single dog he could and saw not a one looked right. *Hope the pup's okay.*

At the street, they turned back to their right, and a block or so later, they turned to their left to go down the main Empire City street. Behind them, the pyramid still had stones being pulled up for construction, and even though he craned his neck to see, he couldn't recognize any of the puller teams including his own.

He followed along, and in a few more minutes, they entered the same building that he'd been in previously, when they'd had that dinner and then been marched out as new slaves.

He felt his hair alongside the nape of his neck stand up, and he was mad, but in shackles and the target of four spears, he followed along meekly. He was ushered into a new room, however. This one had a large round table in the center and a few stewards and yes, more Shieldsmen as well. But no prime disciple.

The black-robed disciple hovered, shifted his weight from one leg to the other, and waited. He looked over at one of the Shieldsmen who was already present in the room and tilted his head.

"No idea, Disciple ... the prime is expecting this prisoner but might be delayed. So we wait," he answered.

They all remained standing and waiting.

In about ten more minutes, a side door opened up, and the prime disciple along with a few of his acolytes came into the room to take seats at the table. Not a one of them paid any attention to those already in the room, Javor noted. No eye contact. No notice at all.

Javor spoke first. "Prime Disciple—I have been unfairly treated and I wish—as an ambassador from the Regime—to register my displeasure with how I've been treated for the past three days," he said, his voice calm but loaded with meaning.

The prime disciple who'd been in conversation with an acolyte started. He was surprised to hear anyone—and even more so, a prisoner—interrupt him and his acolyte.

"Pardon me, slave ... you will speak to me when you are asked to speak. 'Til then, stay quiet," he barked out, his face flushed with anger.

"Not a chance, Prime Disciple. I am an ambassador—we need to remember that first, and that requires that my position here in Empire City be respected," Javor spat out.

The redness on the prime disciples face darkened. "You are a slave. You are lower than any other life form on Ceti4. If I choose to have a Shieldsman spear you right now, you die. Remember that first, slave," he said, and he gestured to have his Shieldsmen step in closer.

Javor stood still. He didn't move and he said nothing. He waited once again.

For more than a half hour, he listened to the prime disciple and his acolytes talk. He listened to them work out a better method of shipping new gas and oil down from their refinery in the north. He listened to them discuss what kind of music to have at some kind of event next week. He listened to what the prime disciple thought of the short list of names presented to him for new Shieldsmen officers. He must have listened to almost another half hour of items that needed input from the prime disciple on various Empire City programs, events, and issues.

And he waited.

Finally, the prime disciple turned to him and leaned back in his chair. "You made a simple mistake, slave. You killed a guard who was your superior," he began.

*Now I know what happened to the guard,* Javor thought.

"I did not do that directly, Prime. I simply was trying to save the water girl from falling off the ramp to the ground well below. That guard was whipping her first—then me," he said as he pointed at the congealed blood scab that hung over his eye and more whip scars on his shoulders too.

"All I did was to stop her from dying, Prime. The guard's death was an accident," he said.

It did sound lame, he thought, but nevertheless, it was the truth.

"I have spoken to other guards and Shieldsmen who were there, policing your pulling team, and what you say is only half true. What you did not say was that you had no need to interfere with the guard and his punishment of that water girl. No need at all. Yet you will pay the price for that act, and Empire City will enjoy watching you in the next Games."

*So, death is the sentence,* Javor thought.

He nodded. "Fine, but I ask that my team not be

affected by this—they were on a break when I acted, and they had no idea as to what I was trying to do. Which was to save the water girl, Prime—is she fine?"

The prime disciple was still just looking at him. "Never mind her. You will be in the next group of slaves to be sent to the Mid-Summer Games. Run fast and true and you might escape—no one ever has, mind you, as our Shieldsmen throw their spears true. You will die, as they all do," he said, and he turned once more to go back to his acolytes and more city issues.

He was marched out and back to his kennel. There, for a change, he was fed a bowl—a good-sized bowl. he thought, of the slave stew that was the usual slave meal. He sat once again on the dirt part of the cage floor, stretched out his legs, and warmed them on the heated concrete in front of him. He watched as close beside him, dog handlers came and took out dogs to be put through their paces. He noted and tried to remember what the commands were that they used in this new language to command the dogs. He watched, he learned, and he listened.

He went back to eating slowly, enjoying the feel of the thin gravy on his tongue and the soft mush of the many vegetables too.

*Should have asked when the next Games were,* he

said to himself as he once again licked a finger that he'd used to swipe around the inside of the bowl...

##### 

Sue finally got some information from a puller guard, but she really had no idea why he'd answered her.

She'd asked him every day about Javor.

Where was he?

What had been done to him?

Why wasn't he here helping to pull?

Couldn't he just let her know anything?

It had taken almost a full week, but eventually the guard she'd been picking on answered her.

"Shut up, slave. You do not need to know that he's going to the Mid-Summer Games. Hope he can run—like it matters," he said as he took a drink from the water girl. His hair, like most of the guards, was long and always sweaty, so he took the bag from the girl and held it up over his head, letting the water pour over. He shook his head and the water cascaded over them all. He gave back the now almost empty bag and went back to sit with the guards on the side of the mezzanine on the ground at the base of the pyramid.

Since Javor had been gone for almost a week, she'd asked those questions. And now she and the rest of her pull team knew that he was going to the

Mid-Summer Games.

She looked over at Toby and said, "And these ... Mid-Summer Games are ..."

He looked away for a moment, shrugged, and then looked back at her. "The games are near the end of the month—the Empire runs them in mid-summer or so, and they are a religious holiday—so to speak. In fact, as we're getting close, I'd say that they always seem to need slaves for the games. Slaves that go ... never come back. It's a death sentence we get to watch from a distance ..." he said, his voice trailing off.

"Until they meet Javor," Wayne said from one side, which didn't get many nods.

Toby looked over to the west at one of the floaters that was going by and said, "That's U-2, one of my favorites. She is quicker than some, not as comfy as the cabins are all inside with no windows—but she can haul big weights of oil barrels." He sighed and squinted in the summer sunlight at the huge black floater as it went by the pyramid, quiet and serene.

"The games are in two days, and that's when they bring all the floaters in and have them tie up right above and around the arena, showing their strength, I believe is what they think they're doing. For me, it's just a chance to see the five of them all together and wishing I was in one," he said and shook his head. "Guess that's one of the first to come in for the Games.

"Would love to get back in the pilot's chair—I'd leave this Empire in my dust," he said as he too drank one more slurp of water from the water girl's bag and handed it back to the youngster.

Sue pondered on that for a moment, while in front of the two teams of pullers, the loaders were getting the next sledge up on the first set of lead rails. Once the sledge was up on that set, a big pull was needed to get the sledge up onto the first rolling log, so there were many slaves milling around, enjoying the usual ten or fifteen minutes of waiting while the next stone was readied to go up the pyramid.

*Javor was going to these games.* She wondered what she—what her cadre team—could do to get that changed or maybe to even escape.

She still had her battery that held the tactical nuke she could simply set off with a time delay, but how could that help them get away and get Javor off the hook too? She shook her head.

She wondered why, as ambassadors, the prime disciple had forsaken all diplomatic rules and made them slaves.

She wondered how she could get her hands on him and make him come around.

"Ready, pullers, on the ropes," a guard called out, and she took her spot on the left side of the team rope, behind Randy this time. Using her right arm, she grabbed the heavy rope and hoisted it up and onto her right shoulder. She took a grip, a good solid grip, with her right hand first and then in front of that with her left hand. She bent over at her waist by about a half and then waited.

"Pull!" came the order, and she and the rest of the pullers on both sides heaved against the massive interior stone that lay on the sledge. Below the very front of the sledge, the rollers were levering in the first log roller, and as they did, the mudders were over at both sides mudding up the three rails they could reach. It took all of them to get the sledge up and onto the first rolling log.

And it took almost a full minute of straining, pulling, prying, rolling, and mudding to get the sledge moving.

And it moved and the rollers tucked in another two or three logs right away to keep the momentum growing.

Sue and the rest of the pullers continued to pull, and the sledge slowly moved along the rails and up the ramp toward the top of the pyramid a long way up…

#####

"Arlington, team A-5 calling in … Arlington … please acknowledge?"

The assault team leader had been trying every hour to reach the Circle of the Regime, but there were problems.

One of the MIA team members had had the battery packs that ran the radio. And he was now most likely dead back in Walkerville at the army base. They had no spares, but that wasn't going to be a problem, it appeared.

One of the team members had some skills when it came to figuring out workarounds, so every hour they stopped. He used wires stripped from under the dash of one of the trucks to connect the truck battery to the radio. Surely not fancy, and it sparked every so often too, but it got the radio up and running.

The Regime still had not answered, but now in the dawn's early hours, someone was on the air.

"Roger, A-5—verifications, please—and page four, please," the voice said, and the team leader opened up the book to page fourteen.

"You add ten to whatever they say," he offered to the rest of the team curled around the open hood of his truck.

He looked down at the page, went to the bottom line of text, and read the line back to Arlington. "Empire planets while humans geared up for ..." and then he said, "Sent."

That was received, and a moment later, an

answering voice came back.

"Team leader, you're verified. What is the result of your mission?"

He reported about the assault on the army base; that they'd lost four men; that they did have six trucks; and that they were on regional roads past the turn off to Lindos. He stated they had an ETA of about three hours depending upon the roads and zombies and all the other factors that might slow them down.

"Oh, bonus, three of them were full of food items, original in their OEM packaging too. I hope," he said with a bit of a grin that Arlington couldn't see, "that everyone likes Twinkies."

A snort came back from the other end.

He listened to what little intel there was on the regional road ahead and what might slow them down. He nodded and then signaled to cut the feed from the battery. They were back on the road in ten more minutes going home.

##### 

The bridge on the *Sophon* was tense.

The ship had been on notice, via Ansible notice, that they were going to get an announcement from Boathi Supreme about their current status on their "ineffective search for the human explorer ship."

At least that's what had come in as a notice.

And now in less than a minute, there would be an Ansible with the supreme commander of Boathi forces.

*Good or bad, they'd know in a minute*, the captain said to himself, and it was out of his hands.

He scratched his ear once again, the rasp loud on the quiet bridge.

Out in front of the ship on the view-screen sat a planet, their number seven on the list of possibilities that the human explorer ship could have reached. And there were no humans here either.

Each day for over a month now, their satellites off each of those seven planets had reported no nuclear power at all. Not a single fissionable event had occurred and they had duly reported that back to the Boathi Supreme command every day as well.

No humans. So, they'd Ansibled back in this morning asking for further assignments and had been told to wait, as there was a message coming soon.

There was a chime on the Ansible console, and the planet on the view-screen changed to the face of the Boathi supreme commander.

His green scales shone. A set of crossed belts ran across his chest, and on the top of each shoulder, the crossed talons, each bright copper colored, denoting the rank of commander, lay there. His face, like all Boathi, was incapable of showing emotion, and as such, it was like it was carved out of emeralds.

He looked out at the *Sophon* captain and shook his head knowing that he would understand this very human indicator of disgust. The Boathi had picked up a few humanisms over the past eighty years of war with them, and this one made the leap between the species. He spoke slowly, distinctly, and yet it rained down on the bridge like a hurricane.

"Captain. Your ship, the *Sophon*, found this human ship—the Drake, I believe, off Arctus4. You attacked and you failed to destroy that ship. She went to light—and you lost her. You did find that she'd gone no further than twenty lights. You searched the seven systems that might be habitable and found no Drake.

"You launched satellites I understand from your reports that have so far said that there is no human ship on any of those seven systems. You have spent now more than five weeks on this, and no human ship has been found. Do I have the facts correct here, Captain?"

Swallowing was difficult, and yet, the captain nodded, swallowed once more, and then said, "Yes, that is the entirety of the facts of this search, Supreme Commander."

He couldn't sweat as the race didn't sweat, but

the smell of fear grew from his body, and the bridge was aware that he was scared of what might come next.

"Your idea, however, that the humans just might have turned off their reactors might have been the thing that saved your career, Captain. Because that was an idea that at least to any Boathi could never have occurred to us. I have checked with Boathi scientists, and what you have countenanced might actually work. Taking a nuclear reactor off-line then letting it sit would have made it invisible to our scans who look for nuclear fission from ships. But as you've indicated, there is no sign of any nuclear power on any of the seven systems."

He looked, as always, like all Boathi , stolid.

He looked, like any superior would, waiting to hear wisdom back to them.

He looked like he believed that his side was the only side that mattered.

The captain thought at breakneck speed and made his pitch. "Supreme Commander, the idea came to me, because we could not find the human ship, this Drake. There was no other way, as the Boathi technology was superior to the humans, that the humans could hide their ship. Damp the reactor to hide it and our scans would never show it, even if it lay right out in the open. So I took the initiative and set up the satellite network to report back to us, should there ever be a reactor that was being restarted. And that is what we have done for the past month, Supreme Commander."

He was nervous, of course, as both his career and his ship were on the line.

The supreme commander nodded his head this time and spoke with a degree of finality. "Exactly, Captain, as you said about 'lying right out in the open ...' You are hereby charged with the duty to go back to each of these systems. To each of the destroyed human planets in same to do a visual scan.

"We don't care what the nuclear scans say anymore. So you go and you look at each city and scour the whole planet. I want that explorer ship found, Captain. Follow the supreme commander's orders. Do it starting today," he finished off.

The captain felt a wave of relief at first, and he almost raised a talon to scratch his ear again until he remembered he was not the senior person present, though the supreme commander was literally almost a thousand lights away.

He nodded. That was one human trait that he too had picked up, and he liked that the Boathi had found some easy ways to show emotion right away.

The view-screen faded out and the supreme commander's image was replaced with the planet below that the *Sophon* was in low orbit around, and the bridge was quiet.

The captain thought about the new mission and then said to the helmsman, "Sub-alternate, let's begin here. I want a low-level flight plan, say, at twenty thousand feet, and let's use a grid pattern to search. I want the scans to indicate all power grids —what comes in and what's going out and any bleeds off grid. I want to find that ship, and if they've not got nuclear power, they still have either battery power or they've plugged into local power. Full power search is what I want," he said, and he tapped his chest with each word.

"Captain, that kind of a power scan of the grids will take, what, weeks perhaps per planet," the sub-alternate said.

The captain nodded and said, "So be it. Let's get down there and begin ..."

FE-CreateSpace

# CHAPTER NINE

Sue nodded to Toby, and he Bruce, and one of Toby's crew began to sing loudly. They sang a song that was an old children's game song with many repeated phrases. The melody was simple and their voices rose to carry it along.

While they did that, Sue and Wayne slid under the last bunk bed before the head, and with them, they took Sue's backpack. Opening it up under the bed's mattress gave them as much privacy as one could expect, knowing that the barracks were most likely fully bugged and recorded. With all of the others, however, sitting on that lower bunk and joining in the singing and all carrying on, they hoped that their presence might not be missed.

Sue's hand dove into the depths of her backpack and came out with the radio and the battery too.

She set them down on the bare floor beside them, then hooked up the single lead from the battery to the radio, and then tried to turn it on. It did not light up, and she knew it wouldn't either, but that was not what this action was for.

A round the bunk, the group was singing a bit louder trying to drown out any radio noise had it turned on, but that was a lost cause, Sue knew. She angled a hand and then her thumb into the back cover of the battery where a hardly noticeable seam lay and pressed it three times.

It popped open and beneath laid a small display screen with some buttons below same. She clicked the one on the far left, and the screen lit and said, "To arm, please choose a detonation time ..." and she grinned.

She began to sing along too. As she clicked the button once more, the screen went dark, and she re-sealed the battery. She stuffed the battery back into her backpack and then rolled to one side to come up from beneath the bunk singing and swaying with the tune.

What the acolyte who saw this might be able to tell had just happened was beyond her.

But she knew that she did have a tactical nuke that was ready to be armed and then detonated.

They said the crater this would leave would be at least a half-mile wide and hundreds of feet deep—

at least the ordnance guides she'd had to read years ago said that. She did hear of this kind of nuke blowing holes that had been much bigger and underwater sending up towering columns of water.

*All I need do now,* she thought, *is figure out how to use this for our advantage and to get both Javor and us away freely.*

*How hard can that be.*

The song kept being sung, and she sang along too, but her mind was stuck on one thought—how to use the nuke to gain the whole team's freedom …

##### #####

The line of slaves slowly moved across the arena floor, carefully raking behind them. Their job was to make the sand as smooth as could be done for the Mid-Summer Games to be held tomorrow. More than a hundred slaves had been pulled off the pyramid building construction sites to help with getting the arena ready.

They'd already put up the flowered decorations and the bunting in sweeping drapes across the tops of the arena walls. The outside bleachers had been completely swept and cleaned and sat ready for the thousands of believers to attend the Games and watch slaves die tomorrow.

At the one side of the arena that was closest to the

city proper, huge temporary poles had been erected with large long ladders that went up to the platform about twenty feet in the air. It was here that the floaters would dock and moor and allow the whole of the Empire to see what the strength of the Empire was all about. They had the only air power on Ceti4, and that alone was enough to boast about. The prime disciple never missed a chance to brag about the Empire.

One of the floaters would actually tie up right at the end of the arena above the doorway to freedom as it was called.

Should a slave, it was said, reach that doorway and climb up the few stairs to that big double set of doors, they would be free and their lives would be spared. Of course, as every believer already knew, not a single slave in the past eight years had made it to the doorway. It was a given that they did try, but they all failed—speared by the best spearmen in the Shieldsmen ranks.

The doorway had been scrubbed clean as well as all the white-washed walls in the whole interior of the arena. All was shining, bright, and ready for tomorrow. There had been an issue with part of the side walls that were taken down to allow the prime disciple and his group better viewing access. But that had been accommodated via a new set of wooden supports that linked their stage from the edge of the interior arena boards. Those boards had been angled through the stage to the mooring pole that held U-1, the biggest and fastest of the floaters to be docked right over their heads.

Big look, big image, and big Empire, everyone would think, and that was what the prime disciple wanted.

The Mid-Summer Games were the last ones that would be held with all of these temporary workarounds in place; in a while, the pyramid would be complete, and then permanent facilities would be designed and built to hold the leadership. That was being worked on currently.

The slaves doing the raking were moving slower than a guard thought they should be, and his whip cracked at one of them as he barked, "Speed up— much more to do today for tomorrow's Games."

The raking did speed up a bit, but each slave was more than focused on getting the sand behind them exactly at the same level as all of the previous feet of now level sand sat at. The job required a bit of skill, and yet it was soon done, and it passed a black-robed disciple's inspection.

Down at the far end of the arena, on either side of the big wide steps up to the only exit, sat fine-meshed cages. Each cage was thirty feet in length on either side. The Empire dogs and their handlers would wait here for any slave that was successful enough to make the stairs, and they would attack the unlucky slave and bring him or her down. No one had ever made it that far, so this was normally just a formality, but the cages had all been cleaned and scrubbed by the slaves. Ten dogs per side were to be housed, and while the fine mesh kept them safe from an errant spear, it provided no safety to any slave unlucky enough to get this far.

Few things did remain, but one of the most important ones was to bring in the shieldsmen and their supplies. The disciple gave that command. and in a half hour, a dozen Shieldsmen came in wheeling a large cart between them that was loaded with brand new spears. They set up the three stations first. They used dye to mark off three large circles on the sand at the starting point only about twenty feet in from the side of the arena against the pyramid mezzanine. It was from within these circles that the three shieldsmen would position themselves to throw their spears at the slaves who were all running for the far door hundreds of feet away.

Beside each of those circles, they erected the pylons and boards that would hold the racks of the fresh new spears. More than one hundred spears fit quite nicely.

Each of the twelve Shieldsmen took a couple of practice hurls, and each was happy with the result.

Their spears shimmered in the bright sunlight as they wafted with power up and then down onto the sand. Each buried their noses more than a foot into the hard-packed freshly raked arena floor—how far they'd enter flesh itself would be looked after tomorrow.

The disciple in charge of the event itself was happy. His report to be given in just a little while to the prime disciple would be positive. All of the odds and ends of the various details of the Mid-Summer Games had been met and successfully quelled.

It was going to be a wonderful Mid-Summer Games.

#####

She sang but she skipped every other line, and Toby and Bruce did as well. Like we're just singing along doing this new roundabout that we'd not yet tried.

She knew this meant that the guards might look at this as slaves gone mad, but she didn't care. They were keeping the watchers and listeners at bay.

It had come to her in the middle of the night, and it had taken the whole day of pulling and waiting and pulling and waiting until the day was over, and tomorrow, they were off to attend the Mid-Summer Games.

She grinned at that, lost her wording, and got a sharp look from Wayne who was standing only a few feet away from the table and last bunk that they usually did their singing from. She waved at him, smiled, and said to Toby at the next open line, "And you can fly one of those floaters, right?" Then she sang the next line as her previous sentence said under her breath was hidden by the loud singing around them.

He nodded as he sang along and tapped his hands on the bunk bed frame at the same time.

She nodded back and spat out quickly, "I have a very small nuke." While it too was covered by the singing, Toby's eyebrows couldn't have raised up higher than what she could see on his face.

He shook his head, waited for the next line, and said, "Really? Still viable?" and that got him a nod in return from Sue.

He smiled and put some extra effort into the line that came along next, as did Bruce who sat on the floor at Sue's feet.

They all sang. The song ended in a few more lines, and then one of the patrollers, Kyle, started up another that they had done just a half hour ago. Why some groups would sing the same song more than once was beyond her, and she just hoped the listeners thought likewise.

Toby filled in a question in the song with "And

you think we can use the nuke to get a floater," and he held up a bobbing hand to show he wasn't finished. And at the next line, he said, "And get us all out of here?" and his hand danced on as he raised up his head to sing even louder.

*Singers, we are not,* Sue thought, *but we can plan with the best of them,* and she nodded back.

The songs lasted a full hour more until they were all tired of just singing.

Wayne suggested that they should offer their choir to the prime disciple—maybe they could sing hymns for the Empire, and that got a laugh from them all.

Working out the details had been tougher than she'd planned, and a couple of items had to happen just so to ensure that the plan could and would succeed.

But Sue too was happy. Their plan had a real chance at success, and escape for them all, including Javor, was at stake.

Life or death … but not life as a slave was how she felt, as did the rest of them.

*Tomorrow. Tomorrow at the Games would tell all.*

# CHAPTER TEN

The rows of believers were long along both sides of the wide bleachers that made up the arena viewing area. It was the opening of the Mid-Summer Games, and all were eager for what was about to occur.

Each was wearing their black robe with the heavy pendant of the copper triangle over top of the circle on their chest. Male, female, child—it made no difference—each was dressed exactly the same. Each sat quietly in their rows, and each row was chanting a variation of the hymn of the Empire as it was called. Everyone knew the chant and the music that came out of loudspeakers that were on almost every block of the ten-block street that ran from the lake at one end to the pyramid under construction at the other.

Behind them, on the actual pyramid itself, although it was unfinished, the leaders of the Empire slowly made their way along the mezzanine area and then over the special walkway to take their place on the stage at about the midpoint of the arena on one side.

The prime disciple, the single man who was the head of the Disciple Apostles, stood and watched carefully as the approaching parade got closer and closer. It was his job to oversee the Empire's religious holidays, and today, these Games were an important part of their holidays. The bleachers would be full of believers, and beside them, the slaves sat in the sun, watching what happened to slaves that were found at fault.

Above the arena were their five floaters, the Empire's best assets, and their job today was to simply sit above the arena and adjoining pyramid and remind the believers that the Empire was the ruling power in the north. Their big black sides were a stark signal that the Empire controlled not only the land but the air as well. All were empty, of course, having been simply moored to the temporary poles that had been erected just for the Games.

Especially today, the Mid-Summer Games holiday.

While he knew this meant the day and night of

today would be a day off for worship, most out in the general population did not know that. To them, it was just a holiday giving them time off from work, and instead they spent the day in religious observance of the equinox themselves. They put on their finest robes and then sat as they were now, singing and chanting the words of obedience and servitude to their God.

His own outfit, a black robe and a big medallion with the pyramid as it would look when it was complete, was as it should be. On his head, he wore the feathered diadem, the bright circle over which the feathered triangle lay centered on his brow.

Behind him but up a step—and he was glad that the step was there—was the Prime Inquisition Board leader, his counterpart in the Forest Empire society who was in charge of all things that were of heresy and religious divergence. He nodded to the man and got a simple nod back as there was no love between them. The Inquisition Board met monthly to test believers and non-believers, and their group had found these slaves wanting. The fact that the Empire needed all the slaves it could get to finish the pyramid was one thing that he was aware of as being important, but the Inquisition Board didn't care. He often shook his head at that.

He stifled a yawn, looked to his left to his acolytes, and noted that they too were softly singing the same hymn. The acolytes to his right were also accompanying the crowds of thousands.

In front of him, the teams of holiday workers had built solid wooden arena walls and had used the sunken slopes there to create an enclosed and fenced large space, two hundred yards long, with bleachers to hold the thousands of believers for the Games.

He thought it looked like an arena of the type he remembered from when he'd been a child those long years ago. Yes, the arena works for me—too bad it wouldn't work for all of them today.

He watched out to his right as the leaders of the parade got closer, prodding the two dozen slaves who actually led the parade as a part of their penance. The slaves who'd done the poorest of jobs, had sloughed off their tasks, or had acted up to the slave overseers were in that group. There were more women this time than last fall but still quite a few men and three children as well.

He watched. From both of the sides of the parade, disciples moved ahead of the slaves up front to get them to funnel into that arena area, right in front of him where he stood. Behind them came a couple of rows of more disciples who pushed the slaves into the arena proper and then gathered them up into three about equal lines. The rest of the parade contingent moved slowly to take up positions around the arena.

He nodded to an acolyte who he'd previously instructed and got the confirmation that the slave from the Regime would be one of the last three to run for his freedom. As if that were true, he thought and smirked to himself.

The prime disciple held out his arms and slowly moved them upward toward the heavens. "We call on our God to accept the non-believers that we now will entrust to his care. And we ask that they be replaced with new non-believers who we can count on to finish our new pyramid to God for the Autumnal Equinox, the most religious day of our year. We ask all of this in the name of our God," he finished off, and as he did so, believers, who up until now had stood at the side of the street in neat and orderly lines, now flooded the arena for the last bleacher seats.

They all rushed to get a seat to view the arena, and most were able to find a seat in the two-hundred-yard-long bleachers. At the closer end to where he stood, there were standing rows at least four or five deep. Every fifty feet or so, a stairway went up the bleachers from bottom to top, and they were half-filled with believers who just wanted to sit and watch.

"Everyone wants to see," he said to himself as he moved backward and stepped up the few steps to sit on his large feathered chair on the stage about a dozen feet above the arena floor.

He nodded to his chief acolyte, and from just below their position, the trumpeters brayed out their notes of opening.

While the arena area below was still a barely finished construction site, it was below grade by about five or six feet, and that gave the watchers a great view. Maybe we should add that to the drawings, the prime disciple thought as the final preparations were taking place below.

At the far end of the enclosed arena, a line of the Empire Shieldsmen entered, and they marched in perfect unison. Each was, as usual, stripped to the waist and so well muscled that just seeing one of them identified them as a member of the arm of the Empire that enforced its rules. They did not wear the robes that the rest of the believers wore; instead, they wore a large sash around their waist on top of the short leggings and boots all in black. Some had had tattoos done on their arms and chests while others had piercings, but no one would ever think was any of these men were anything else but a Shieldsman.

As they entered the arena area, a vast cheer went up from many around the walls of same, and some even yelled for their choice of who would be the best today. They marched and curried favor as they moved the whole length of the arena to stand behind the rows of slaves back on his right at the start of the arena course.

The prime disciple had no favorite. It did not matter to him at all who did the best today ... yet he would be one of the first to admit that the Shieldsman known as Oskar was one of the best he'd ever seen. Oskar could hurl his spear with deadly accuracy almost three-quarters of the length of the arena, and when he was one of the three Shieldsmen hurling, the slaves had no chance at all.

As the Shieldsmen took up their positions, three of them went to stand beside the three lines of the slaves. Each of the Shieldsmen had been given a spear about three meters in length weighing about a pound and a half. There was a coiled rope to act as a handle about mid-way down the shaft, and the long point was smooth, ultra-sharp, and barbed as well.

Each of the Shieldsmen hefted their weapon, trying to get familiar with it. At the far end of the arena was the large set of stairs leading up to the double doorway out of the enclosed arena area. Just inside stood a row of Shieldsmen, all armed with the same spears and all at ease. It was their job to mop up the non-survivors, but the real interest was back down in the arena.

The rows of dogs in their cages were there as

final backup. While no one had ever made it out of the arena, should someone get that close, they'd face the dogs. He smiled at that. Empire dogs were loyal and faithful, yet when ordered to attack, they were vicious hell-hounds.

The trumpeters rang out another peal of notes, as the prime disciple nodded to an acolyte. Within the arena at the head of each of those three lines of slaves, a line disciple there unfettered a slave, got them up on their feet, and pointed all the way down the arena floor to that open doorway in the distance.

"If God wants you to live, you will only find your life on the other side of that doorway," the three line disciples screamed at the three slaves.

The three slaves began to run toward the far doorway, and the trumpets blared to start them off. The shieldsmen stepped forward, and each waited a moment before they drew back, ran, and then launched their spears into the air. Each spear flew at breakneck speed, and each impaled the running slave that was the Shieldsmen's target, and the slaves dropped to the sand floor, their blood leaking out onto the white sand. There were huge cheers, laughter, and cries from the host of believers, as some had wagered on their favorite Shieldsman and won, and yet others had lost.

From the end of the arena, the mop-up Shieldsmen ran down. With quick thrusts, they ended the lives of the speared slaves and then dragged them off to lay at the sides of the arena.

"Three down and more to go," the prime disciple said to himself, and he nodded once again to his chief acolyte. The thing was that as the remaining slaves could see what was happening, the second ones learned not to run the route to the door in a straight line. This is where the event gets interesting, he thought.

As the next three slaves were unfettered and then stood up, he noted that one was a teenager who was looking around frantically. "Dad ... Dad, where are you?" he yelled at the top of his cracking voice, but there was no answer.

As the line disciples urged these three new slaves to make for the doorway and their freedom, two of the adults—a man and a woman—took off running but dodging first this way and then another. After more than forty yards, even the prime disciple could see they had fallen into a pattern of those dodges, and as he thought that, the next Shieldsmen saw it too and threw not where the slave was at that moment but where they'd be after the next dodge. The man and woman flopped to the sand. The spears struck them both right in the back, and the sand was bloody once more.

The teenager did the same thing but did not fall into a pattern. In fact, he was doing quite well, moving across the arena in wide swaths as he dodged first one way, then the same way again, then back, and then away. The spear of a Shieldsman fell onto the sand as it missed him completely.

But moments later as all three of the current crop of Shieldsmen retrieved new spears, they laid out a spread pattern, and the teenager took a spear to his left thigh, impaling him to the sand. He crawled, or tried to, as the doorway was only fifty yards away, but the mop-up Shieldsmen quickly dispatched him and the sand got bloodier.

The crowd screamed, "Oskar, Oskar ... Oskar, Oskar ..." and he took a bow, as he had gotten the youngster.

The prime disciple knew that once the dodging appeared to also not to work, most of the slaves usually just ran straight, knowing that the death they faced was best done soonest.

##### 

As the line in front of him got shorter, and he realized *he'd be one of the last three to run,*

Javor made more of those mental check-boxes trying to find a way out of this mess.

*The Shieldsmen all take about seven seconds to get the second spear into the air, if the first one misses. Check.*

*Twice, the one in front of the line that he was in had*

*taken three spears to kill the running slave. Check.*

*The best spearman is beside me to my left, so when I run — I'd better avoid that area if I can. Check.*

*The stage holding the prime disciple is approximately twelve feet up off the arena floor. Check.*

*The slave area on the left, same side as the stage, is where Sue and the cadre would be milling about. Check.*

*The running slaves do not work together to evade the spears. Check.*

*The spears that are thrown just stick in the sand 'til the mop-up crews come out to remove them and the slave bodies. Check.*

Ahead of him, there was now only one slave left, and he knew the information he'd gathered was not enough to find a way out. Perhaps enough to shake up the Empire, he mused as the only slave ahead of him ran off to his death.

It did take the Shieldsman on his row three spears to get the slave, who'd tried the deke and fake method of running but to no avail. As the mop-up crew came out to finish them off, that meant that eighteen slaves had died today.

Javor said to himself, *twenty-one might be the number of slaves, but there'd be more. At least one more.*

As the line disciple on his line approached him, he waved the man away, moved up to stand in the circle at the front of his line, and smiled. The trumpets sounded and then the whole arena got quiet, as the prime disciple rose and moved to the front of the stage.

"We now have in the middle circle one of the so-called ambassadors from the Regime—that group of unbelievers to our south. He will run alone and die today for us to show them and the rest of Ceti4 what we think of non-believers. I hereby also offer that the Shieldsman who shows this slave what we think of him will also win a promotion to the rank of Shieldsman Superior. Good luck, Shieldsmen," he said as he continued to stand right there at the front of the stage.

Javor nodded. *Okay, so now the game's afoot.*

He bent over to take a solid starting stance.

The trumpets blared, and he ran out about twenty feet, then left, then left again, and then right, and then he stopped cold. Above his head, three spears hit the sand well ahead of him, as the stopping of his run had been so unexpected.

He smiled as he tore toward the closest spear, and then picking up same, he turned and threw with all his best javelin technique at the Shieldsman behind him on the right. That man wasn't even watching as he was grabbing another spear off the rack, so Javor knew exactly where he'd be. The spear caught him full in the back of the neck, pinning him to the sand below.

The whole arena cried out as he turned and then

loped once again toward the far doorway.

*Still got my javelin chops,* he said to himself as he drifted off to the left in his run. But their spears are just a bit light—caught that one in the neck when I'd aimed at the man's full back. As he ran, he glanced back over his right shoulder at the one called Oskar, the better spearman, and noted that he'd just let go. He dove to the sand on his right and rolled and rolled.

The spear came close but missed him, as he rolled. He got up and grabbed the spear. The other spear caught him in the left calf, passing just over his large muscles, and the blood poured out as the crowd began to cheer for their Shieldsman who'd just thrown.

He turned back and noted that both of the Shieldsmen were watching him, holding out hands waiting to be fed a new spear, and not turning their backs to go to the rack to get their own. "Smart," he said to himself as he gauged the distance between himself and the stage.

No way to take the thirteen steps he was trained to use when he did the high jump. His approach, he knew, would require a certain shape or curve, the right amount of speed, and the correct number of strides. The approach angle was also critical for optimal height, and in this case, it was a dozen feet. *Jumped just about that back in competitions,* he said to himself as he tucked the spear behind his left arm.

He ran and used that alien tissue super right knee at the last second to jump.

The prime disciple sneered at him, believing he was too high and safe.

Javor planted that right foot on the sand, knowing that it was not the best take-off surface, and he launched himself up and up and up …

# BONES: A Cliffhanger Series...

Yes, this is a book in our new BONES series, that is a Cliffhanger series.

If you're upset by the ending, my apologies...but wait'll you find out what happens to Javor and the Prime Disciple in the next book entitled Castle Magic.

Cliffhangers I am told sometimes generate a review that the reader is upset...and I hear you. But please do note that the blurb up front, taken directly from the book's Amazon page says right up front that the BONES series of books are Cliffhanger books...

Hopefully, you'll also be pleased to note that I promise that within a month of publication of each BONES book, the next one in the series will be published and thereby solve any worries you might have as to Javor and his adventures on Bones!

Read! Enjoy....and see you on Bones soon!